CLAIMED

—

TRACY WOLFF

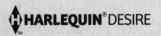 HARLEQUIN® DESIRE

ISBN-13: 978-0-373-73408-5

Claimed

Printed in U.S.A.

Isabella was somehow even more beautiful than he remembered.

And probably more treacherous, Marc reminded himself as he fought for control over his suddenly rampaging emotions and libido.

It had been six years since he'd seen her.

Six years since he'd held her, kissed her, made love to her.

Six years since he'd kicked her out of his apartment and his life.

And still he wanted her.

It came as something of a shock, considering he'd done his best not to think about her in the ensuing years. Sure, every once in a while something would come up and her face would flash through his mind. He'd be reminded of the scent, the taste, the feel of her. But through the years those instances had grown fewer and further between and his reaction to them—and her—had dimmed. Or so he'd thought.

All it had taken was a glimpse of her through the small window to throw him right back into the seething, tumultuous heat that had characterized so much of their relationship. At that moment, he hadn't cared about the future, or his family's company, which he had sacrificed so much for through the years. He hadn't cared about anything but getting to her...

* * *

Claimed is part of the Diamond Tycoons duet—
Marc and Nic Durand are ruthless,
sexy and powerful, and only the women they love
can tame them.

Tracy Wolff collects books, English degrees and lipsticks, and has been known to forget where—and sometimes who—she is when immersed in a great novel. At six, she wrote her first short story—something with a rainbow and a prince—and at seven, she ventured into the wonderful world of girls' lit with her first Judy Blume novel. By ten, she'd read everything in the young-adult and classics sections of her local bookstore, so in desperation her mom started her on romance novels. And from the first page of the first book, Tracy knew she'd found her lifelong love. Tracy lives in Texas with her husband and three sons, where she pens romance novels and teaches writing at her local community college.

Books by Tracy Wolff

Harlequin Desire

The Diamond Tycoons
Claimed

Harlequin Superromance

A Christmas Wedding
From Friend to Father
The Christmas Present
Beginning with Their Baby
Unguarded
Deserving of Luke
From the Beginning
Healing Dr. Alexander

Visit the Author Profile page at Harlequin.com
or tracywolffbooks.com for more titles.

One

Isabella Moreno froze in the middle of her lecture—in the middle of a sentence, really—as the door in the back of her classroom opened and the president of the Gem Institute of America walked in. But it wasn't the presence of Harlan Peters that threw her off her game. She was a damn good professor and she knew it; a visit from her boss was no big deal. No, it was the tall, dark and silent man standing next to him that struck fear into her heart even as he sent shivers up and down her spine.

Don't forget gorgeous, she thought as she forced herself to continue her discussion of the cutting and polishing of off-shape sapphires. Her graduate students had begun turning to look at what had distracted her and it was only a matter of seconds before she would lose the attention of every female in the vicinity. Already, there were twitters and giggles coming from various corners of the room, and they didn't even know who the mystery man was yet.

Not that she did, either. Not really. Oh, she recognized him. It was hard to be in the gem industry for any length of time and not be able to identify Marc Durand, CEO of the second largest diamond exporter and jeweler in the country. His too-long black hair, bright blue eyes and fallen angel face were hard to miss…and even harder to ignore. But the look on that face, the glittering contempt in those distinctive eyes and the derisive twist of those full lips was not something she was used to seeing from him. They turned him into a stranger.

The Marc she knew—the Marc she'd once loved—had looked at her only with tenderness. With amusement. With love. At least until the end, when everything had fallen apart. But even then he'd shown some feelings. Rage, hurt, betrayal. It had nearly killed her to see those emotions on his face, and to know that she was responsible for them.

But the look on his face now—the derision, the scorn, the *ice*—turned him into someone new. Someone she didn't recognize; someone she certainly didn't want to know.

When they'd been together, their relationship had been characterized by heat, so much heat she'd often wondered how long it would take before she got burned. The answer, it turned out, had been six months, three weeks and four days, give or take a few hours.

Not that she'd been counting.

And not that she blamed him for how things had ended. How could she when the way things had gone down—the way the two of them had self-destructed—had been almost completely her fault?

Oh, he could have been kinder. She was the first to admit that tossing her onto the streets of New York City in the middle of the night, with nothing but the clothes on her back, was a hideous thing to do. But it wasn't as if she hadn't deserved it. Even now, there were nights she lay awake staring at the ceiling and wondering how she could have done what she had done. How she could have betrayed the man she'd loved so completely.

But that was the problem. She'd been caught between two men she loved, adored, would have done anything for, and because of that, she'd ruined everything. She'd known her father had stolen from him and though she'd tried to convince her dad to give the gems back, she hadn't told Marc who the thief was until it was nearly too late for him to salvage his business. And then she'd made the situation worse by begging Marc not to prosecute, and by admitting that when she'd sought him out at the gala where they'd first met she'd been planning to steal from him, too. Her plans had changed—her life had changed—once she'd spoken to him, once he'd looked at her with those crazy blue eyes of his, but—

Isabella shied away from the painful memories instinctively. Losing Marc in the middle of everything else had nearly brought her to her knees six years before. She'd be damned if seeing him again, after all this time, did the same thing. Especially here, in the middle of her first graduate seminar of the day.

Forcing her wandering mind back to the task at hand, she was mortified to realize every student in the class was looking between her and Marc. As was the college president. Despite the years that had passed, the connection between them was obvious, the tension a live wire that threatened to spark at any moment. Determined not to let that happen, and not to let the atmosphere in the room get any more awkward than it already was, Isabella forced herself back to her task.

The next part of her lecture was on the world's most famous sapphires and their locations. When she got to the part about the theft of the Robin's Egg Sapphire—one of the most expensive and sought after gems in the world—she did her best not to look at Marc.

But in the end, she couldn't help it. Her gaze was drawn to his, the magnetic force of his personality—his will—allowing her to do nothing else. She froze the second their eyes connected, the sardonic look he leveled at her as sharp as the finest hewn diamond. Marc knew what had happened to the Robin's Egg. He'd made it his business to know before he'd confronted her in their bedroom—his bedroom—that long-ago night.

"We're sorry to interrupt, Dr. Moreno," Harlan said from his spot in the back of the classroom. "I was just showing Mr. Durand around the campus. He's agreed to teach a miniseminar on diamond production starting in a few weeks and I wanted to give him the lay of the land. Please, carry on with your lecture. It's fascinating."

But it was too late for that. All around her, students murmured excitedly. Not that she blamed them. It wasn't every day that one of the world's largest producers and brokers of responsibly sourced diamonds agreed to speak to a bunch of first year graduate students. Still, she was the professor here. This was her lecture. She needed to regain control, if not for the class—which was only half-over—then because she refused to let Marc Durand have the upper hand for one second longer.

He'd taken everything from her. Or, to be completely honest, she'd given everything to him, only to have it all tossed back in her face. She'd deserved it then, and had paid for it royally. But that had been six years ago. Since then, she'd moved across the country and built an entirely new life for herself. She'd be damned if she let him come in here and screw that up for her, too.

Refusing to let Marc see just how much his presence

here messed with her mind, she continued on with her lecture. Eventually the students settled down again and Marc and Harlan slipped out a lot more unobtrusively than they'd entered.

If anyone asked her what she spoke about for the last twenty minutes of class, Isabella wouldn't have been able to tell them. Her mind was far away, wrapped up in a past she regretted bitterly but couldn't change and the man who had altered the entire course of her life. She must have covered pretty well, though, because the students didn't call her on anything. Then again, they'd all been so enamored of Marc Durand that they probably weren't focusing on what she had to say, anyway.

Finally, the interminable class drew to an end and she dismissed her students. It was her usual habit to hang out in the classroom for a few minutes to give the students an opportunity to ask questions or chat her up about whatever was on their minds. But today she didn't have it in her to stay there one second longer than absolutely necessary, not when her insides felt scraped raw and she was certain any wrong move would shatter the peace she had worked so hard to achieve. The peace she had finally found.

Scooping up her books, and the papers her students had turned in that day, Isabella made a beeline for the door. She was parked around back. If she could get to the side exit, she could be in her car and off campus in less than five minutes. Then it would be just her and the convertible, the infinite ocean to her left as she followed the winding, waterfront freeway home.

Except she never got to her car, never even made it to the side door she was so desperate to reach. Instead, a strong, calloused hand grabbed her elbow as she tried to hurry down the back hallway. Though she was facing the other direction, she didn't need to see him to know who had grabbed her. Her knees turned to gelatin at that first touch, her heart beating wildly out of control. There would be no escape then. No drive by the ocean. No chance to put her thoughts in order before this confrontation.

Not that she was surprised. From the moment she'd looked up and seen Marc in the back of her classroom, she'd known this was inevitable. She'd simply hoped to put it off a little, until she could think about him without losing her ability to breathe. Of course, she'd already had six years and hadn't been able to change that, so another couple of days probably wouldn't matter.

Besides, if he was going to destroy everything she'd tried to build for herself with her new name and new identity and new, law-abiding life—then she might as well find out right now. Worrying about it would only make her crazy.

Bracing herself, she put on her best poker face before slowly, slowly, turning to face him. And if her knees trembled as she did, it was nobody's business but her own.

She was somehow even more beautiful than he'd remembered. And probably more treacherous, Marc reminded himself as he fought for control over his suddenly rampaging emotions and libido.

It had been six years since he'd seen her.

Six years since he'd held her, kissed her, made love to her.

Six years since he'd kicked her out of his apartment and his life.

And still he wanted her.

It came as something of a shock, considering he'd done his best not to think about her in the ensuing years. Sure, every once in a while her face would flash through his mind. Something would remind him of the scent, the taste, the feel of her. But through the years those instances had grown fewer and farther between and his reaction to them—and to her—had dimmed. Or so he'd thought.

All it had taken was a glimpse of her gorgeous red hair, her warm brown eyes, from the small window embedded in the classroom door to throw him right back into the seething, tumultuous heat that had characterized so much of their relationship. He hadn't cared about the president of the college, hadn't cared about the future he had so carefully mapped out for Bijoux, the family company he had sacrificed so much for through the years. He hadn't cared about the workshop GIA had hired him to teach now that he had moved Bijoux's headquarters to the West Coast. To be honest, he hadn't cared about anything but getting into that classroom to see if his mind was playing tricks on him.

Six years ago he had kicked Isa Varin—now, apparently, Isabella Moreno—out of his life in the cruelest manner possible. He didn't regret making her leave—how could he when she'd betrayed him so completely?—but in the time since, he had regretted how he'd done it. When he'd come to his senses and sent his driver to find her and deliver her things, including her purse and cell phone and some money, she had vanished into thin air. He'd looked for her for years, simply to assuage his conscience and prove to himself that nothing untoward had happened to her that night, but he'd never found her.

Now he knew why. The very passionate, very beautiful, very bewitching Isa Varin had ceased to exist. In her place was this buttoned-down professor, her voice and face as cool and sharp as any diamond his mines had ever produced. Only the hair—that glorious, red hair—was the same. Isabella Moreno wore it in a tight braid down her back instead of in the wild curls favored by his Isa, but he would know the color anywhere.

Black cherries at midnight.

Wet garnets shining in the filtered light of a full moon.

And when her eyes had met his over the heads of her students, he'd felt a punch in his gut—in his groin—that couldn't be denied. Only Isa had ever made his body react so powerfully. So instantaneously.

He'd ditched the GIA president as soon as he could, then had rushed back to make sure he caught Isa before she could slip away. And still he'd almost missed her. Not that he was surprised. She did come from a long line of cat burglars, after all. He knew from experience that nine times out of ten, if she didn't want to be caught, she wouldn't be.

As he waited for her to speak, he couldn't help wondering what he was doing here. Why he'd caught up with her. What he wanted from her. Because the truth was, he didn't know. He knew only that seeing her, talking to her, was a compulsion he couldn't resist.

"Hello, Marc." She raised her face to his, her voice and countenance as composed as he had ever seen them. He felt a brief lick of something deep inside—a feeling that made him uncomfortable for the simple reason that he couldn't identify it. So he ignored it, concentrating instead on her as their gazes met in a clash of heat and memories.

One look into her eyes—dark, endless pools of melted chocolate—used to bring him to his knees. But those days were long gone. Her betrayal had destroyed any faith he might have had in her. He'd been weak once, had fallen for the innocence she could project with a look, a touch, a whisper. He wouldn't make that mistake again. He would satisfy his curiosity, find out why she was at GIA, and then he would walk away.

As he stared down at her, those same eyes were alive with so many emotions he couldn't begin to sort them all out. Her face could be as unemotional as she wanted it to be, her body as ice-cold as it had once been fiery-hot, but her eyes didn't lie. Isa was as disturbed by this chance meeting as he was.

The realization had something relaxing deep inside him and he felt the power shift sizzle in the air around them. She'd once had the upper hand in their relationship because he'd trusted her blindly, loved her so deeply that he had never conceived that she would one day betray him.

But those days were long gone. Isa could pretend to be the straitlaced, boring gem professor all she wanted. He knew the truth and he would never be stupid enough to let his guard down around her again.

"Hello, Isabella." He made certain his face showed only sardonic amusement. "Fancy meeting you here."

"Yes, well, I go where the jewels are."

"Don't I know it?" Deliberately he glanced at the wall across from them, where one of the most expensive opal necklaces ever created was displayed behind glass. "The president tells me you've been teaching here three years. Yet there've been no heists. You must be slipping."

Her eyes flashed furiously, but her voice was controlled when she answered, "I'm a member of the GIA faculty. Helping to ensure the safety of every gem on this campus falls in my job description."

"And we all know how seriously you take your job… and your loyalties."

The mask cracked and he got a glimpse of her fury before she shored her defenses back up. "Is there something you need, Marc?" She glanced pointedly at his hand, which was still wrapped tightly around her elbow.

"I thought we could catch up. For old times' sake."

"Yes, well, it turns out the old times weren't all that good. So, if you'll excuse me—" She started to wrest her elbow from his grasp, but he tightened his fingers. Despite the anger that ran through him like molten lava at her words, he wasn't ready to let her go just yet.

"I don't excuse you." He put a wealth of meaning behind those four words, and saw with satisfaction that she hadn't missed his point.

"I'm sorry to hear that. But I've got an appointment in half an hour. I don't want to be late."

"Yeah, I hear fences take exception to lateness."

This time the cool facade did more than crack. She shoved against his chest with one hand at the same time she wrenched her elbow from his grasp. "Six years ago I put up with all your vile insinuations and accusations because I felt like I deserved them. But that was a long time ago and I'm done now. I have a new life—"

"And a new name."

"Yes." She eyed him warily. "I needed distance."

"That's not the way I remember it." She'd chosen her father over him, even after the old man had stolen from him. It wasn't a slight Marc had any intention of forgetting.

"No surprise there."

The insult—in her words and her tone—had him narrowing his eyes. "What's that supposed to mean?"

"Exactly what it sounded like. I'm not big on subterfuge."

Though it made him sound like an arrogant ass, he couldn't help throwing her words back at her. "Again, that's not the way I remember it."

"Of course not." She straightened her spine and lifted her chin. "Then again, you've always been more about perception than truth. Right, Marc?"

He hadn't thought it was possible for him to get any angrier. Not when his stomach already churned with it, his jaw aching from how tightly he was clenching his teeth.

Then again, she'd always brought out strong emotions in him. At one time, they'd even been good emotions.

Those days were long gone, though, and he wouldn't let her drag him back there. The Marc who had loved Isa Varin had been a weak fool—something he'd sworn he'd never be again as he'd watched security escort her from his building.

"That seems an awful lot like the pot calling the kettle black, Isabella." He put added emphasis on her new name, could see by the darkening of her eyes that the irony wasn't lost on her.

"On that note, I think it's time for me to leave." She started to step around him, but he blocked her path. He didn't know what was driving him, only that he wasn't ready to watch her walk away from him again. Not when she looked so cool and collected and he felt…anything but. And not now that he'd finally found her.

"Running away?" he taunted. "Why am I not surprised? It does run in the family, after all."

For a second, hurt flashed in her eyes. But it was gone so fast he couldn't be sure he hadn't imagined it. And still, a little seed of guilt lingered. At least until she said, "Whatever you're doing here, whatever you think you're going to get, isn't going to happen. You need to get out of my way, Marc."

It was an ultimatum, for all that it was said in a polite tone. He'd never been one to respond well to such things. Still, her fire excited him, turned him on, as nothing had in six long years. His reaction pissed him off, but he'd be damned before he let her see that. Not when she was there, in front of him, when he'd been so certain he would never see her again. He wasn't ready to let her walk out of his life for another six years, not when he still had so many unanswered questions. And not when he still wanted her so badly that every muscle in his body ached with it.

So instead of doing what she asked, he lifted a brow and leaned casually against the cool, tile wall behind him. Then asked the question he knew would change everything. "Or what?"

Two

Isa stared at Marc in disbelief. Had he seriously just asked her that? As if they were kids playing a game of double dog dare and it was now her turn to up the ante? Too bad for him that she'd given up childish games the same night she'd walked forty city blocks through sleet and freezing rain without so much as a coat to shield her from the weather. She'd moved past that night, had made a new, better life for herself here under a name no one in the industry could trace to her father. There was no way she would let him mess all that up.

"I don't have time for this," she told him with an annoyed snarl. "And while I'd like to say it was nice seeing you again, we both know that I'd be lying. So—" she gave him a mock salute "—have a nice life."

Turning on her heel, she once again started down the empty hallway. This time she only made it a couple of steps before he wrapped one large, calloused hand around her wrist and tugged her to a stop.

"You don't actually think it's going to be that easy, do you?"

His rough fingers stroked the delicate skin at the inside of her wrist. It was a familiar caress, one he'd done so often in their months together that she'd felt his phantom stroking in that exact spot for months—years—after they'd broken up. Even now, with everything that had passed between them, with the power he held to ruin her life all over again, her traitorous heart beat uncontrollably fast at the light touch.

Furious with herself for being so easy—and at him for being so damn appealing—she yanked her arm from his grasp with more force than his gentle hold demanded. She ended up stumbling back a couple steps before she could catch herself, a reaction that just annoyed her more. Why was she constantly making a fool of herself in front of this man?

Infusing her voice with as much frigidness as she could muster, she forced herself to meet his gaze. "I don't know what you're talking about."

Those glorious eyes of his mocked her. "Still a good liar, I see." He reached out and ran a hand over her braid. "Nice to see some things haven't changed."

"I never lied to you."

"But you didn't tell me the truth, either. Even when doing so would have saved my company and me one hell of a lot of time, money and embarrassment."

Old guilt swamped her at his words. She tried to push it away, but it was too constant a companion for her to do anything more than invite it in like she always did. Still, she refused to take all the blame in this situation. Not when the tender man she used to know had vanished like so much smoke. "Yes, well, you seemed to have landed on your feet."

"As have you." He very deliberately glanced into the classroom she had just vacated. "A professor at the GIA, one of the world's leading experts on conflict-free diamonds. I have to admit, when you disappeared so completely, I thought you'd decided to follow in your father's footsteps."

Isa drew in a sharp breath, horrified that his words still had the ability to hurt her, even after all this time. "I'm not a thief." She'd meant the words to sound scornful, but her voice broke in the middle of the sentence.

His look darkened and for a second, just a second, she thought he would reach out to her. To touch her like he used to—with so much tenderness that she couldn't feel anything but cherished. Every nerve ending in her body tingled at the thought and despite his hurtful words—despite everything that had passed between them—she almost melted into him. She had to lock her knees, in fact, to keep from leaning on him as she had so many times before.

But then he cleared his throat and the spell was broken. All the bad memories poured into her, overwhelming the good from one breath to the next. Tears burned behind her eyes, but she refused to shed them. Refused to be so weak in front of him. Besides, she'd already cried all the tears over him she ever would. Their relationship was in the past and she was going to keep it there.

She stepped back and this time he didn't pursue her. He just watched her with a smirk on his face. She supposed that meant the next move was hers. So be it.

Taking a deep breath, she looked him square in the eyes and did the only thing she knew how to do at this point. She opened herself up and told him the truth. "Look, I know you want your pound of flesh, and God knows, you deserve it. I'm sorry, so, so sorry, for everything my father put you through. But he's gone now and there's nothing else I can do to make things right. Can you accept my heartfelt apology and then we can both move on? You teach your class, I'll teach mine. And the past can stay dead."

He didn't move, didn't so much as blink, but Isa swore she felt him recoil at her words. She waited nervously for him to say something, anything, but as the seconds ticked by and nothing was forthcoming, she grew more and more nervous. To be watched by Marc Durand was to be watched by a hungry predator, one whose teeth and claws, speed and intellect, gave him an advantage over every other species on the savannah. Or the beach, she admitted ruefully, looking out at the ocean through the windows at the end of the hall.

She shifted under his scrutiny, uncomfortably aware that the last time he'd spent this much time looking at her she'd been naked and begging for him to make love to her. And while sleeping with him was the farthest thing from her mind right now, her traitorous body still remembered all the pleasure he'd brought her. Pleasure she had never seen the likes of before or since.

Her nipples hardened at the thought and her cheeks burned in humiliation. He hated her, was disgusted by her very presence. She'd spent six years in a new life, trying to forget him. And still she couldn't help fantasizing about what it felt like to be in his arms. Marc was an incredible lover—passionate, unselfish, fun—and the months she'd spent with him had been the best of her life.

But they'd been followed by the worst, lowest months, she reminded herself bitterly. She needed to remember that. Just because her body was still attuned to him, still wanted him, didn't mean the rest of her did. Sexual chemistry had only gotten them so far, after all.

He still hadn't said anything and the sensually charged

silence between them grew more and more uncomfortable—at least on her part.

Isa squared her shoulders, cleared her throat and said, "I really am late. I need to go."

She hated that it sounded like she was asking his permission, but the connection that had sprung up between them was such that she wasn't sure she'd be able to walk away if he didn't do something to help her sever it.

"There's a cocktail party tonight," he said abruptly. "In the gem gallery."

Surprised by the bizarre change in subject, she nonetheless nodded. "Yes. It's the spring faculty mixer."

"Go with me."

Isa shook her head, certain she must have heard him wrong. Marc couldn't possibly have asked her to attend the faculty cocktail party as his date? Why would he? Unless he planned to humiliate her there in front of all her colleagues.

The Marc she used to know, the one she'd been hopelessly in love with, would never do anything like that. But she hadn't seen that man in six long years and this one—hard, angry, uncompromising—looked like he was capable of anything. She wanted no part of him, no matter what her pleasure-starved body said.

"I can't."

"Why not?" It was obvious he didn't like her answer.

"I already have a date." The words poured from her lips before she had a clue she was going to say them. And while they weren't a lie, they weren't strictly the truth, either. She and Gideon, another professor, had made plans to go together weeks ago. They were just friends, though, and she knew Gideon wouldn't mind if she canceled on him.

But she would mind. She could barely stand the fifteen-minute conversation she and Marc were having in the hall. She couldn't even imagine what would happen to her—or the new identity she'd worked so hard for—if she spent an entire evening in his company. If she gave in to the attraction that still flared between them. Besides, she might be insane enough to still be attracted to him, but her days of being his whipping girl were long over. She was nobody's masochist.

"Who is he?" The words grated out from between his clenched teeth.

"Gideon. No one you know. But maybe I'll see you there."

She forced a smile she was far from feeling. She even gave a little wave before she started down the corridor for the third time in the past twenty minutes. This time he let her go.

By the time she opened the side door and stepped into the early spring sunlight, she'd almost convinced herself she was happy about that fact.

"Who pissed in your cornflakes?" Nic demanded.

Marc looked up from his computer with a scowl. Per his usual modus operandi at Bijoux's new California headquarters, his little brother had barged unannounced into Marc's office. Normally Marc didn't mind, but right now, just hours after that conversation with Isa, dealing with Nic was the last thing he wanted to do. Not when his brother was unusually perceptive—not to mention his wicked and slightly strange sense of humor. It was a dangerous combination, one that usually required Marc to be on his toes if he had any hope of staying one step ahead. And today, he didn't have it in him to even try.

"I don't know what you're talking about."

"Sure you do. Look at your face."

"That's pretty much impossible considering there's no mirror in here."

"Why, oh why, did I get stuck with a brother with absolutely no imagination?" Nic demanded, looking upward as he did—as if he expected the universe to answer his question. Frankly, Marc thought Nic had a better chance of finding the answer written on the ceiling than waiting for divine intervention, but he didn't mention that. It would only give Nic more ammunition.

Instead, Marc answered the question. "So that you'd look like the fun brother."

"It was a rhetorical question. Besides, I don't have to look like the fun brother. I *am* the fun brother," Nic told him with a roll of his eyes. "But, fine. You can't see your face. I can. And let me tell you, you look like someone…" He paused as if searching for the perfect descriptor.

"Pissed in my cornflakes?"

"Exactly. So what's up? More trouble with De Beers?"

"No more than usual."

"The new mine?"

"Nope. I just heard back from Heath and things are going well. Despite it being brand-new, we should be turning a very tidy profit by the fall."

"See? Who says you can't make money *and* responsibly source diamonds?"

"Greedy bastards with no heart or social conscience?"

Nic snorted. "Again, it was a rhetorical question. But good answer, anyway."

"That's why I get paid the big bucks."

Marc turned back to his computer, tried to concentrate on the spreadsheet that was open on the screen. Normally, this stuff was like catnip to him, but today looking at the production values of the various mines was nothing but an annoyance. Especially when he couldn't stop thinking about Isa—and the mystery man who was escorting her to the cocktail party. Was he a friend? A boyfriend? A lover? The last thought had his hands curling into fists and his teeth clenching so tightly that he could almost feel the enamel being ground away.

"See, there!" Nic said. "That's the look I'm talking about."

"Again, can't see it."

"Again, I can, so tell me what's causing it. If we're not losing money and we're not yet in our annual power struggle with De Beers, then what the hell has you so freaked out?"

Marc glared at him, offended. "I don't get freaked out."

"Well, you sure aren't freaked in." Nic crossed to the bar in the corner, pulled a couple of sodas out of the fridge and tossed one Marc's way.

"What the hell does that even mean?"

"It means I'm going to keep bugging you until you tell me what's wrong, so you might as well spit it out. Otherwise, you'll never get back to that spreadsheet of yours."

"What makes you think I'm looking at a spreadsheet?"

"Face it. You're always looking at a spreadsheet." Nic settled back into one of the visitors' chairs and kicked his feet up onto Marc's desk. "Spill."

Marc pretended to focus on his computer screen, but Nic didn't get the hint. Or if he did, he totally ignored it. Silence stretched between them, broken only by Nic's occasional swallow and the low, clicking sounds that came from Marc's gritted teeth. Finally, in the hopes of saving himself a hefty dental bill, Marc did what his brother asked and spilled.

"I ran into Isa today."

Nic's feet hit the ground with a thud as he sat straight up. "Isa Varin?"

"Isabella Moreno now."

"She's married?" He whistled low and long. "No wonder you're in a foul mood."

"She's not married!" Marc snapped out. "But even if she was, it's no business of mine."

"Oh, certainly not," Nic mocked. "You've just spent the last six years dating every redhead you could find in a ridiculous attempt to replace her. But her marital status is none of your business."

"I've never—" He broke off midrant. He wanted to tell his brother that he was dead wrong, that Marc hadn't done anything of the sort. But as he thought back over the last few women he'd dated, Marc realized that Nic might have a point.

He'd never noticed before but all the women in his life *were* redheads. Tall, slender redheads with delicate bones and great smiles. Hell. Had he subconsciously been trying to find a replacement for Isa all these years? He'd never thought so, but the evidence was hard to ignore. Damn it.

"So, why the name change if she isn't married?"

He didn't know, but he was going to damn sure find out. Still, he told his brother what she'd told him. "She said she wanted to start over."

Nic made a sympathetic noise. "I bet."

He didn't like Nic's tone. "What's that supposed to mean?"

"What do you think it means? Things didn't exactly end well between you. I know when you kicked her out, it was what you felt you had to do."

"It was what I had to do! Do you really think there was another option?" Marc waved the question away before Nic could answer it—they'd been over this ground hundreds of times since that night. "Still. I've paid a hell of a lot of money to private investigators through the years.

You would think one of them would have turned up this name change."

"Not if she didn't do it legally."

"It'd have to be legal. She's employed under the name."

"Have you forgotten who her father is? With the kind of contacts he had, she could buy herself a whole new identity without breaking a sweat."

"Isa wouldn't do that." But even as the words left his mouth, Marc wasn't so sure. What his brother was saying made a lot of sense. After all, she'd lied before. Stolen before. How else could the daughter of a world famous jewel thief—a woman who had been a thief in her own right—end up teaching at the world headquarters of the Gemological Institute of America—even if she was one of the best in her field? Working there, she had access to some of the finest gems in the world—they rotated through the institute on loan on a pretty regular basis, after all.

And while she might not be a thief, her father's reputation would be more than enough to keep the doors at GIA firmly closed to her. Unless she had done exactly what his brother surmised. Because if she'd changed her name legally, there was no doubt that the detectives Marc had hired to look for her in those first couple of years would have caught it.

"So, how's she doing anyway?" Nic broke into Marc's musings. "Is she okay?"

"She's fine." Better than fine. She'd looked amazing—healthy, happy, glowing even. At least until she'd seen him. Then the light inside her had died.

"I'm glad. Despite the debacle with her father—and despite what happened between the two of you—I always liked her."

So had he. So much so that Marc had asked her to be his wife, despite his determination before he'd met her to never marry. It wasn't as if his parents had set such a great example for him and Nic in that department.

"So, did you ask her out?"

"Did I—? Are you kidding me? Aren't you the one who was just reminding me how badly things ended between us?"

"You were a bit of an ass, no getting around that. But Isa has a big heart. I bet she'll forgive you—"

"I'm not the one who needs forgiveness in this equation. She nearly ruined all our plans for Bijoux!"

"Her *father* nearly ruined all our plans, not her."

"She knew about everything."

"Yeah, but what was she supposed to say? 'By the way, honey, that diamond heist you're so worked up about? The one that might bankrupt your business? I think my daddy did it.'"

"That would have been nice. So that I didn't have to hear about it from the head of our security team."

"Cut her a break. She was twenty-one years old and probably scared to death."

Marc frowned at him. "You're pretty damn understanding all of a sudden. If I remember correctly, you were calling for her head when everything was going down."

"Her father's head," Nic corrected. "I thought he should fry for what he did, but you were the one who refused to press charges. And who pulled every string you could to get him out of trouble. Hell, you're still paying back favors from that whole debacle."

Nic was right. Marc was—and the favors were often uncomfortable ones. More than once, he'd wondered what the hell he'd been thinking. Why had he worked so hard to keep Isa's father out of prison after what the man had done? But then he'd seen her face in his mind's eye—pale, drawn, terrified—and known that he hadn't had a choice.

Getting up, Marc crossed to one of the two picture windows that formed the outside walls of his corner office. Beyond the glass, he had a gorgeous view of the Pacific Ocean as it crashed against the rocky shoreline. He studied it for long seconds, letting the roll of powerful waves calm some of the annoyance—and confusion—inside of him. Moving Bijoux's North American headquarters to San Diego six months ago was one of his smarter moves. He'd done it because of the proximity to the world headquarters of GIA, but access to the ocean was a very nice side benefit.

"He was a sick, old man. Salvatore was dead before the year was out, anyway. He didn't need to spend the last couple months of his life in a cell."

"You did that for Isa, and because underneath that crusty exterior you've actually got a soft heart—"

"Crusty? You make me sound like I'm ninety!"

"You said it, I didn't." Nic's smartphone alarm went off and he sprung to his feet. "I've got to go. There's a marketing meeting starting in five minutes that I want to sit in on."

"Everything going okay with the new campaign?" Marc asked. He was the CEO of Bijoux, the guy who handled all the business stuff—governmental contracts, mining, employees, distribution. But his brother was the creative genius in the family. He handled marketing, public relations and sales. Anything that had to do with Bijoux's public image. And he did it brilliantly, something Marc appreciated because it gave him time to concentrate on what he loved best—growing his family's gem company into the largest socially and environmentally responsible diamond company in the business.

"It's going great," Nic said dismissively. "I just like to

be at all the meetings to hear the ideas, see what's going around. Get a sense of the zeitgeist, I guess you could say."

"And they call me the control freak in the family?"

"Because you are. While I am merely conscientious." Nic crumpled up his empty soda can and shot it toward the recycle bin in the back corner of Marc's office. "Yeah, baby, nothing but net."

Marc bit his tongue to keep from telling Nic that there was no net. God forbid he get another lecture on not being the "fun" brother.

Nic made his way toward the exit, then stopped at the doorway and turned back to Marc.

"Seriously, bro. Fate's given you another chance with Isa. You should take it."

"I don't believe in fate. And I don't want another chance with her."

"You sure about that?"

"Positive." After everything that had gone down between them? The last thing he wanted was to give Isa another shot at screwing up his business...or his heart.

Did he want to sleep with her again? Hell, yeah. What man wouldn't? She was beautiful when she was aroused. Not to mention sexy as hell—especially when she screamed his name while she came. Being with her had been the best sex he'd ever had.

Then again, she'd always been more the type to make love than have sex. He'd loved that about her when they'd been together. Now, however, it was nothing but a pain in his ass—not to mention other, more notable parts of his anatomy. He didn't do the whole tenderness thing anymore.

"Well, then, forget about her," Nic told him practically. "The past is dead. You've both moved on. Keep it that way."

"I intend to."

And yet, Marc couldn't help thinking about Isa—and about her date to the party that night. *Gideon*. Just the name set his teeth on edge. What kind of name was Gideon, anyway? Who the hell was he? And what the hell did he want with Isa?

An image of her standing in front of her classroom flashed through Marc's mind. Her eyes alight with the thrill of talking about her favorite subject, her skin flushed and glowing. Her miles of red hair locked down in that ridiculous braid, her gorgeous body hidden, and yet revealed, by the tailored pants and turtleneck sweater she'd been wearing.

When he'd known her, she'd been all warm, sweet passion—for life, for gems, for *him*. Now she was a contradiction, a bunch of stopping-and-going that, combined, made for an even more intriguing woman. One that he couldn't help wanting despite his anger, and her betrayal.

No, Isa hadn't been eager to renew their acquaintance that afternoon. But he'd seen the way she looked at him, the way she swayed toward him when he touched her. Maybe getting her into bed again wouldn't be nearly as challenging as it once had been. The thought made him smile. Because once he got her there, he would take her—over and over and over again. Every way a man could take a woman.

He'd get her out of his system once and then, finally, he'd be able to put her—and all their unfinished business—behind him once and for all.

Three

He was there. Marc. Though she hadn't run into him yet, Isa had felt him watching her from the moment she and Gideon had walked in the door of the faculty mixer. It had always been that way with them—she couldn't help but sense Marc whenever he was anywhere close to her.

"Can I get you a drink?" Gideon asked, his mouth inches from her ear. She knew he did it because it was hard to hear in the gallery—overlaying the soft music was the sound of a hundred voices, all vying to be heard—but still, feeling his warm breath so close to her cheek and neck unnerved her. Made her feel a little uncomfortable.

Which was stupid. Gideon was her friend and occasional movie/mixer date. It had been that way since they'd met three years before and never once had he given any indication that he wanted more. They were buddies, pals, each other's port in a storm. So why was she suddenly feeling so awkward around him?

A shiver ran down her spine, and with it came the answer to her question. Because Marc was there, watching her. And though she hadn't so much as caught a glimpse of him, she knew he wouldn't like the fact that Gideon was so close to her, his face next to hers, his hand resting softly at the center of her back.

As soon as the thought came, she beat it down. She and Marc had been over for six long years. He probably couldn't care less that she was here with Gideon—any more than she cared who he was with. Any feeling she had otherwise was probably just a leftover from when they had been together. Back then, Marc had been extremely possessive of her. But then, she'd felt the same way about him.

"Isabel?" Gideon's smooth voice dropped an octave as concern clouded his bright green eyes. "Are you all right? You've seemed off ever since I picked you up."

He was right. She had been off—and not just for the past half hour. She'd been feeling strange ever since her encounter with Marc in the hallway earlier that day. And now, knowing that he was here made her feel a million times more off-kilter.

To make up for it, she flashed Gideon a wide, warm smile. "I'm sorry. I've just been caught up in my thoughts. But I'll put them away for now, I promise."

He grinned back at her. "Careful with that smile, woman. It's a lethal weapon." His own grin faded. "You know, if you need anything you can count on me, right?"

"Of course. But I'm fine. I swear." She leaned into him, gave him a brief kiss on his cheek. "Though I am thirsty."

"Your usual?" he asked, steering her toward a group of colleagues that they were both friendly with.

"That would be perfect."

After depositing her among their friends, Gideon took off toward the bar. Isa tried to relax, to enjoy the ebb and flow of the quick-witted conversation she was usually right in the middle of. But she couldn't. Not when it felt as if Marc's eyes were boring holes right between her shoulder blades.

"So, how was the ballet you went to last week?" asked Maribel, one of the other professors at the GIA. "I'm so sad I had to miss it."

"Yes, well, I think an appointment with your obstetrician trumps an afternoon at the theater," Isa told her. "But the ballet was great. It was student written and performed, but you would have never known it. The San Diego Ballet Academy has a really good program."

"Well the next time one of those afternoons of student work comes along, I want in. Even if it means I have to get a babysitter." Mirabel softly rubbed her swollen tummy.

"How is the baby? And how are you feeling?"

"The baby's fine and I feel gigantic. I can't believe I have two more months of this to go."

"Hopefully it will go fast," her husband, Michael, told her as he gently rubbed her back.

She snorted in response. "Really? And you know this because you're carrying around a beach ball in your stomach?"

They all laughed, even Michael, and Isa felt the tension finally begin to drain from her shoulders. Yes, Marc was here but there was no reason they had to do anything more than exchange a polite hello. If that.

Gideon came back with her drink—a crisp, cold glass of Pinot Grigio—but before she could do more than smile her thanks at him, she heard the dean's voice right behind her. "Good evening, everyone. I'd like to introduce you to the newest guest lecturer on our faculty."

The man hadn't even said Marc's name before her stomach dropped to her toes. Because, really, who else would the dean be personally escorting around the cocktail party besides the CEO of the second largest diamond conglomerate in the world?

Her friends welcomed Marc easily, much to her dismay. Not that she could have expected any differently. They were a fabulous, friendly, nosy bunch of people and any new lecturer—especially one of Marc's stature—would be of interest to them.

He fit in well, of course. Remembered everyone's name on the first go round. Told a quick story with a punch line that had everyone roaring with laughter. Asked appropriate questions that gave everyone in the group a chance to show off a little.

In other words, Marc was in perfect social mode—the one he slipped into so easily when he was doing the party circuit and the one she'd never been able to perfect, no matter how hard she'd tried. When they'd been together, she'd wanted to be the fiancée he could be proud of. She had tried so hard to be as charming and at ease as Marc was in the various social situations he'd thrust her into. But the fact of the matter was, she was shy.

She loved talking to her students, loved talking to her friends. But making small talk with strangers? Struggling to come up with something to say that would hold people's attention—especially the people Marc introduced her to? Those situations had made her intensely uncomfortable to the point that she would have anxiety attacks hours before they went out.

She'd never told Marc, of course. Had never wanted him to feel ashamed of her or find her lacking. She'd loved him so much, had been so desperate to be Mrs. Marc Durand, that she would have done anything he asked of her. Had done anything, everything—except betray her father.

And that one decision, that one stand against Marc, had cost her everything.

Anger churned in her stomach, combined with the wine and nerves until she felt more than a little nauseous. Gideon noticed that something was wrong right away. He put an arm around her waist and pulled her against him.

"You okay?" he asked softly, his lips pressed against her ear so no one else could hear. He was one of the few people she'd ever trusted with her social anxiety. It was one of the reasons he insisted on being her escort to parties, and why he always made sure she was with friends before he left her side to get drinks or anything else.

"I need some air," she whispered back.

"The terrace is open. I'll take you."

"No, I'm fine." He'd been enjoying the conversation immensely—the talk of ballet had turned into a spirited discussion of San Diego's arts scene—and it wasn't fair to take him away from it. "Stay. I'll be back in a couple of minutes."

He frowned. "Are you sure?"

"Positive." She leaned into him a little more, gave him a quick hug. Then excused herself to use the ladies' room.

As conversations ebbed and flowed around her, Isa made her way to the wide-open doors at the end of the room. They let out onto the terrace that overlooked the ocean and as she got closer she could feel the sea breeze sweeping through the room. It was a little chilly, a little salty and exactly what she needed to help her get her head back on straight. And to forget about Marc and the painful past she had no hope of changing.

Slipping around the last group of people, she walked straight out to the darkest part of the terrace. Bracing her hands on the iron fence that closed it in, she closed her eyes and let herself breathe. In, out. In, out. In, out. Already, she felt calmer. More in control. She wondered how long she could stay out here before Gideon came looking for her.

She was gorgeous. Dressed in a simple purple sheath that stood out like a beacon amid the sea of black cocktail dresses, she was as sexy, as sensual, as he'd remembered. More so even, maturity lending a lushness to her face and figure that hadn't been there before.

It was a lushness that clown Gideon had noticed. One he'd taken every chance to brush against or touch or hold. Standing there, doing nothing, while that bastard had pawed Isa had been one of the hardest things Marc had ever done. Especially when he'd wanted nothing more than to smash his fist into the jerk's face.

Only the fact that Isa seemed to like Gideon's touch had stopped him, even as it had cranked his anger into a lethal place. One where the six years between now and when she'd been his had melted into nothing, like snow on the first warm spring day.

He watched her weave her way through the bodies, watched as she slipped out onto the terrace, finding a dark corner with only a little light to stand in.

Watched as she took a deep, shuddering breath. Then another and another.

Her beautiful breasts trembled against the deep V of her neckline and Marc's fingers itched—ached—with the need to touch her there. To hold the warm, firm weight of her in the palms of his hands while he kissed, licked, sucked her nipples until she orgasmed.

It had been one of his favorite things to do when she'd been his.

As he stood there, watching her, an image came to him. One of Gideon on his knees in front of her, pleasuring her the way Marc used to. Rage exploded within him, turned his voice harsh and tinted his vision with red. Or maybe that was green.

Within seconds he was next to her. "Who is this Gideon guy to you?" The question came out before he even knew he was going to ask it.

Isa's eyes flew open and she whirled to face him, one shaky hand pressed to her chest.

"I'm sorry. I didn't mean to startle you."

"What are you doing out here?"

"I followed you." He stepped forward, ran his fingers down the sweet softness of her cheek.

"Why?"

He ignored her question, focused instead on the sudden increase in her breathing. She was either nervous or aroused. Or maybe both. He wanted to revel in her reaction, probably would have, if he hadn't been struck by the sudden realization that her response might be for Gideon instead of him.

"Who is that guy to you?" he asked again.

"Gideon?"

He didn't like the way she said the guy's name, all soft and familiar. It pushed at him, made him snarly. And more determined than ever to have her in his bed again. "Yeah."

"He's my escort. And—and my friend."

Her voice broke as he slid his hand from her cheek to her jaw to the pulse that fluttered wildly at the base of her neck. "Is that all?"

She wet her lips with her tongue and he nearly groaned. It took every ounce of control he had not to lean forward and brush his own tongue against hers.

"Is what all?" She was breathless now, her chest rising and falling unevenly.

The knowledge that she wanted him, too, sent a shot of lust straight to his groin. He stepped closer, brushed her body with his even as he circled her neck with his thumb and fingers. It wasn't a threat or an attempt to intimidate. No, it was simply a gesture of the possessiveness ripping through him like a freight train, one he couldn't have stopped even if he'd wanted to.

And he didn't want to. Not when need for Isa was a fire in his blood, a haze in his mind.

He leaned forward until his lips were only an inch or so from hers. "Gideon. Is he just a friend? Or is he more?"

"G-Gideon?"

He liked the confusion in her voice, liked that she couldn't remember who he was talking about. "The guy who brought you here." Marc leaned closer still, brushed his lips over the corner of her mouth. "Are you with him?"

Isa shuddered, trembled, against him. "No."

The denial came out as a whisper, but it was good enough for him. More than good enough as her skin flushed and her nipples peaked against his chest.

"Good," he said, right before his mouth closed over hers.

Four

The kiss was as much about possession as it was about pleasure.

It had been six long years since he'd touched her, since he'd held her, since he'd licked his way across her full pink lips, but, in this moment, in his mind, she was still his.

At the first press of his mouth against hers, Isa's lips parted on a gasp. He took instant, ruthless advantage, thrusting his tongue into the deepest recesses of her mouth. Her hands came up to his chest and he thought, at first, that she was going to push him away. Just the idea upset him more than he wanted to admit. He prepared for it, for the torture that would be letting her go. But then her hands clung instead of pressed, tangled in his shirt and held him close. It was all the permission he needed.

He brought his hands to her face, cupped her jaw. Stroked his thumbs along her cut-glass cheekbones. And kissed her as if he'd been dying to kiss her for all these years.

He *plundered* her.

Sweeping his tongue along her own, stroking and circling, teasing and tasting, he coaxed her into opening a little wider, letting him in a little deeper. She did, and he swept in, taking more of her. Taking everything she was offering and demanding more.

He licked his way across her lips, down the inside of her cheeks, over the slick roughness of the top of her mouth. She moaned then, a soft, breathy sound that shot straight through him and made him harder than he'd been any time in the past six years. Harder than he'd been any time since he'd last held her in his arms.

With that thought in his mind and desire pounding through his gut, he tilted her head to gain better access. And then it was on.

Their tongues tangled, slipping, sliding, stroking their way over and around and under each other. He sucked her tongue into his mouth and relished the way her body arched, the way her hips bumped against his, the way her fingers clawed at him, scratching him through the thin silk of his dress shirt.

He used to love the little pricks of pain, and the knowledge that he would carry her marks for hours, sometimes days. It was a blow to find out he still felt that way. That he still wanted her brand on his body—and his brand on hers—as much as he ever had. Or it would be a blow, he figured, as soon as this kiss was over. For now, he couldn't think about it. Couldn't think about anything but her and the feelings rushing between them. Because he didn't have a choice, he gave himself over to it all. Gave himself over to Isa.

How could he not when the kiss, when *she*, was a strange mix of soft and sharp, poignant and desperate.

The familiar and the exotic. He wanted her—and whatever she would give him—more than he wanted air.

His head was spinning by the time she pulled away. She didn't go far, just broke off the kiss and stood there panting, her forehead resting against his. He let her catch her breath, and dragged precious oxygen into his own overworked lungs, giving his overheated body a chance to calm down. Then he claimed her mouth again.

It was even better the second time.

Her lips were warm and swollen and she tasted so good—like fizzy wine and the sweetest summer blackberries. And the sea. Cool and clean and so, so wild. But then, she always had.

So much about her had changed since he'd last been with her, he'd been afraid that taste had, too. To find out that it hadn't—it nearly brought him to his knees. Instead of letting it, he kissed her again. And again. And again. Until her skin was hot and flushed against his palms. Until he was rock hard and aching against her. Until their lips were bruised and swollen and tender, so tender..

And then he kissed her some more.

And she let him. She let him kiss her, let him touch her, let him in when he'd spent so long thinking that it would never happen again. That she would never open herself to him and that, if she did, he would never trust her enough to let her.

But this wasn't about trust, he told himself as he continued to take everything she had to offer and push for more. This wasn't about love. It was about need. About chemistry. About a past that burned hotter between them than any jewelry forge ever could.

His mouth was nearly numb by the time she finally broke the kiss. This time she didn't stay in his arms, resting against him. Instead, she shoved him away, hard, then turned to face the ocean. He gave her space, and just watched, fascinated, as her shoulders trembled, as she struggled desperately to get herself under control.

He wished her luck. God knew, he had absolutely no control when it came to her. He never had.

"Don't ever do that again."

It was an order, delivered in a voice that still shook from pent-up desire.

"Never do what?" he asked, turning her around so he could see her face in the shadowy darkness. Her eyes were huge; her pupils wide with passion and seeing her like that sent another shock wave of need through him.

"Never do this?" he asked, stepping so close that every breath she took pressed her breasts against his chest. "Never touch you?" He brushed his knuckles against her jaw, then slid them down, until his open hand rested on her collarbone, his fingers splayed gently against her neck. "Never kiss you?" Her skin was soft and warm against his lips as he kissed a line from her temple to her cheek to the corner of her mouth.

Then he pressed his mouth to hers, pulled her lower lip between his teeth and bit down gently.

Isa's hands slid up his back to tangle in his hair as she made low, urgent sounds deep in her throat. Her lips parted on a shallow exhale as her body arched against him. It was all he could do not to groan. Not to take her right there against the iron railing of the balcony.

"Never want you?" His hand was on her waist, and he slid it down to mold her behind, to press her hips against his while his other hand slid down to cup her breast through the thin, silky fabric of her dress. "Because, I have to say, I think the ship has sailed on that. For both of us."

"Marc." His name was a broken breath on her lips—a prayer, a curse, an absolution, a condemnation. He didn't know which—nor did he care, he assured himself. All that mattered was having her again. He'd spent the past six years thinking about touching her, dreaming about taking her over and over until his mind was calm and his body was finally sated.

Maybe then he could find some peace.

"Let me have you," he whispered in her ear even as he rolled her nipple between his thumb and forefinger. "I'll take care of you, make you feel so good—"

Isa shoved against him, hard. She was a little thing, slender, with tiny bones—but she was a lot stronger than she looked.

"Marc, no!" She twisted her face to the side and shoved again. "Stop."

No. Stop. He hated those two words, almost as much as he hated being told what to do. But they were nonnegotiable, the words and the sentiment behind them not open for discussion when they fell from a woman's lips. And so he stepped back, letting his hands fall away from her lush, inviting curves.

"I know what you're doing," she said. Her eyes were wild, her voice shaky.

"Do you?" he murmured. "Do you really?"

"You're trying to embarrass me at work. You're trying to ruin everything and I'm not going to have it."

He didn't even try to hide his insult. "Embarrass you? Kissing me embarrasses you?"

She must have sensed the danger in his voice, because she ran a nervous hand over her hair while the fingers of her other hand played with her locket. "Don't get all macho and insulted on me," she told him, exasperated.

"I don't do macho," he said, disdain in every syllable.

She snorted. "You don't have to 'do' it. Every cell in your body is alpha and controlling and if you don't know that, you're even more deluded than I thought you were. But, be that as it may, I'm not going to stand out here and be your toy for one second longer. This is a work function for me and, unlike you, I don't have a trust fund and a diamond company to fall back on if I lose my job for inappropriate conduct. This career is all I have and I'm not going to let you ruin it, the way you ruined—"

She broke off before she finished the sentence, moving around him in a quick and desperate attempt to get to the door.

He grabbed her elbow, but it was his will much more than his gentle grip that kept her in place. "The way I ruined our relationship?" he asked silkily. "Because the way I remember it, you did that all on your own."

"I have no doubt that's exactly how you remember it." She glanced pointedly at his hold on her, then pulled her elbow out of his grasp before he could say another word. "Which is how I know you're doing this just to mess with me, to get me in trouble. But I'm not having it. I don't ever want you to touch me again. Go back to whatever you were doing before you decided that humiliating me was your best bet. Or better yet, go to hell."

She moved past him then, disappearing back into the party in a swirl of purple silk, Chanel No. 5 and righteous indignation.

He wasn't sure what it said about him that it was the latter that turned him on the most.

She was insane. Or in the middle of a psychotic break. Or having a stroke. She didn't know which of the three she was suffering from, but it was definitely one of them. There was no other explanation for what had happened on that balcony. No other explanation for why she had fallen into Marc's arms—and onto his lips—as if it had been six minutes since they'd last been together and not six years. Or as if he hadn't sent her packing in the cruelest manner possible.

She understood sexual attraction—when they'd been together, she and Marc could barely keep their hands off each other. But shouldn't that attraction be grounded in respect or love or something other than the intense dislike and distrust they now had for each other?

And still she'd let him kiss her. She'd let him touch her and stroke her and bring her way too close to orgasm. It was ridiculous. Worse, it was self-destructive. She was ashamed of herself. Ashamed of her body for responding so readily to him after everything he'd done to hurt her. After everything she'd done to hurt him, too.

As she walked through the party back to Gideon, Isa could feel Marc's eyes following her. She didn't need to look to know he was running his gaze over her back, her backside, her legs—and then up again. The weight of his stare was a physical touch—like an electric shock all over her body.

By the time she got to Gideon, she was shaking with reaction and self-recrimination. Though she knew the smart thing for her career was to stay at the party, drinking champagne and waiting for her turn to chat up the president of the Gem Institute, the truth was she didn't have it in her to be in this room for one more minute. She had to escape, now, before she freaked out in front of all these people. Or before she threw herself at Marc and begged him to take her right here, in the middle of the crowded gallery.

Just the thought that such a thing was possible had her all but running the last few feet to Gideon. Had her putting her hand on his arm and leaning in so that her lips were only inches from his, so he could hear her in the loud, crowded room. Had her begging off the rest of the night, telling him she'd catch a cab home because she wasn't feeling well. She was pretty sure her sickly pallor and trembling hands lent credence to the assertion.

Gideon, bless him, immediately put his drink on the nearest table and said, "Poor Isa. Let's get you home, then." He slid his arm around her waist to lend extra support and—after making his excuses—steered her toward the door.

"You don't have to come with me," she told him a little frantically. "It's just a headache. I can get myself home."

"Don't be ridiculous! I brought you, I'll escort you home. Besides—" he shot her a goofy grin "—that place was getting damn stuffy, damn fast. In fact, we could say you're rescuing me instead of the other way around."

"I think we both know that's not true," she said, pressing a kiss to his cheek. "But I appreciate the sentiment… and the ride home."

As soon as her lips left Gideon's cheek, she knew the kiss had been the wrong thing to do. She couldn't see Marc, but she could feel the crackling fury of his disapproval all the way across the room. With her back turned. And her attention determinedly fixed somewhere else.

She stiffened her shoulders and tried not to let his reaction bother her. After all, it wasn't as though she was using Gideon to try to make him jealous—it wasn't as though it had even occurred to her that he would *be* jealous. But now that she could feel him seething from across the room, she couldn't help but wonder what this whole thing looked like to Marc. One minute, she was letting him violate her on the balcony and the next minute she was snuggling up to Gideon.

Not that it mattered what Marc thought, she promised herself as she allowed Gideon to propel her toward the exit with a proprietary hand on her lower back. She'd told Marc that what had happened on that balcony wouldn't happen again, and she'd meant it. She'd let him destroy her once. No way would it happen again. It didn't matter if she was still attracted to him, didn't matter if there was unfinished business between them. She was no longer the love-struck girl she'd been six years ago, willing to risk anything and everything for a chance to be with him.

No, life had taught her a lot of hard lessons in the intervening years and she'd ended up building an entirely new life for herself. One she was proud of. One that meant something to her. One that Marc would be only too happy to ruin as completely as he'd ruined her old one.

She couldn't let that happen. Not when her job—and her reputation—were all she had.

Five

The ride home with Gideon was easy. But then, everything was easy with him. There was no smolder. No dark past that tainted every interaction, no love or hate to color the way they looked at each other. The way they were with each other. No, she and Gideon had a comfortable friendship, one built on shared interests, lively conversations and similar senses of humor.

And never had she been more grateful for that than she was right now, as he pulled up in front of the small house she'd bought for herself when she'd moved here four years ago.

Gideon walked her to the door, but he didn't linger. Didn't expect an invite inside or even a good-night kiss. Instead, he hugged her and dropped a quick kiss on her forehead. Then, with a murmured, "Feel better," he was gone. And she was alone.

Thank God.

Ignoring the way memories of Marc simmered right under the surface, she changed out of her dinner clothes into yoga pants and a black tank top. Then she poured herself one more glass of wine and settled on the couch to watch television and try to forget her disaster of a day.

Except she'd barely streamed the opening credits to her current favorite TV show before there was a knock on her door. Figuring Gideon had come back because she'd left something in his car, she opened the front door with a grin. "What did I forget this time? If you want to come in, we can share a bottle of—"

Her voice cut off as it registered just who was standing on her front porch—and he definitely wasn't Gideon.

"What are you doing here?" she demanded. "And how did you even find out where I live?"

"I followed you."

"You followed—Jesus. Stalk much?" She started to close the door in his face.

His hand flashed out, holding the door before she could get it more than halfway closed. "I've spent the last six years looking for you."

For a second, she was sure she had heard him wrong. After all, the last thing Marc had said to her was that if he ever saw her again, he'd make sure she and her father both ended up in prison.

But the look on his face—a little guilty, all annoyed—told her she had heard correctly. And that he hadn't meant to blurt out the truth like that. But now that he had, she wanted to know—"Why? Why would you do that?"

"It was a shitty thing to do."

"I believe we've already covered how you feel about what I did—"

"No. I mean what I did. Tossing you out on the street like that, having security escort you from the building with nothing… I regretted it almost as soon as it happened. I went outside the building, tried to find you. Went to your apartment, but you never went back there. I was worried that something had happened to you because of me."

It was the last thing she'd expected him to say, the last thing she'd ever expected to hear from Marc Durand. For long seconds she could do nothing but stare at him as she tried to absorb the words. She didn't want them to matter, didn't want anything to get in the way of her ability to tell him to go to hell once and for all. After all, the words— and the sentiment behind them—were six years too late.

And still she felt something melt inside her. For six long years she'd carried a twisted mess of betrayal and pain, regret and rage. Every bit of it had his name on it and no matter how many times she'd tried to let it go, no matter how many times she'd tried to move on, it had been there, choking her. But now, somehow, with just a few words, Marc had loosened its stranglehold on her. She could take what felt like her first deep breath in forever.

"I'm sorry," he continued, and it sounded like he was swallowing razor blades. Not that she was surprised. In her experience, men like Marc didn't apologize often.

And now that he had…she had a choice. She could tell him to go to hell and slam the door in his face or she could accept his apology. Since she'd always understood why he'd done what he had—her father *had* stolen from him, and in begging Marc to spare him, she had chosen her father over Marc—there really was only one choice she could make.

Opening the door a little wider, she stepped back. "I just opened a bottle of Pinot Noir. If you're interested."

"I'm very interested." His voice was dark, wicked. She felt the heat of it in her stomach and her sex.

It made her nervous. Made her sweat, despite the chill

of the air-conditioning. "It's probably not as fancy as the wines you're used to," she told him as she entered the kitchen and poured him a glass of her favorite Pinot. "But I like it."

He took the glass, drained it in one long sip. Put it on the counter behind him.

"Okay, then. Do you want m—"

He moved to cage her against the cabinet, an arm on either side of her and his long, lithe body pressed against her own. "I didn't come for the wine, Isa."

"Obv—" Her voice cracked, so she cleared her throat. "Obviously."

"I didn't come to apologize, either. I'm glad I did, but that's not why I'm here."

"Marc." The word was low, broken. "I don't think—"

"Don't think," he said, cupping her face in his big, worn hand. "Just listen." He leaned down until his lips brushed, soft as butterfly wings, against her jaw.

"I wasn't messing with you on the balcony earlier." His breath was hot against her ear. "I wasn't trying to humiliate you at work."

Her nipples beaded despite her earlier resolve to never let him make her feel like this again. "It felt like that to me."

"I know. And that's my fault, too." His mouth skimmed across her jaw, his tongue darting out to taste the corner of her mouth. "Wrong time, wrong place."

He licked his way across her lips, soft and delicate and oh so coaxing. She gasped at the first touch of his tongue on her lower lip and he took instant advantage, licking inside to stroke her.

"My only excuse," he said, in between each dark and wicked kiss, "is that even after all this time, you make me crazy. You make me forget where." His other hand cupped her breast through the thin cotton of her shirt. "You make me forget when." He stroked his thumb around her areola.

Her heart was beating too fast, her chest heaving with each ragged breath she sucked past her too-tight throat. Still, she managed to force out the question she was desperate for an answer to. "Do I make you forget who, as well?"

"I've never been able to forget you, Isa. And believe me, I've tried."

The words stung, of course they did. But there was an honesty to them that echoed her own experience, that had her weakened defenses crumbling into dust.

She could blame her surrender on the wine or the loneliness or the shock of seeing him after all this time. But the truth was, she wanted him. She'd always wanted him. And if this night, this moment, was all she'd ever have of Marc Durand…well, it was a more fitting goodbye than the last one they'd shared.

And so she didn't fight him when he moved to trail kisses down her throat. Instead she let her fingers tangle in his dark, silky hair even as she tilted her head back to give him better access.

"Your heart is beating so fast," he murmured against her skin.

"It's been a long time since—" She forced herself to stop before she revealed too much.

But he wouldn't let her off the hook that easily. "Since what?" he asked between pressing kisses across the upper slope of first one breast and then the other.

She couldn't tell him the truth, didn't want him to know just how much she'd once loved him—or just how long it had been since she'd made love to someone. "Since you've touched me. Our chemistry was never in question."

Then, to keep him from digging any deeper into what was a very sore subject, she ran her hands over his chest.

He'd discarded his jacket and tie before coming to her door, so all that was between her fingers and his hot skin was a thin piece of dark blue silk the same color as his eyes.

He was as powerfully built as ever—maybe more so—and she'd be lying if she said she didn't want to see him naked. Didn't want to feel the heat of his skin, the resilience of his muscles, under her tongue.

But sanity finally intruded—in the form of his long-ago rejection that was still fresh in her mind. She didn't think she'd be able to go through that a second time. At least not if she wanted to come out anywhere close to whole. So instead of unbuttoning his shirt as she longed to do, instead of slipping her hands inside the midnight-blue silk and stroking his pecs, his six-pack, the V-cut that had always made her mouth water, she forced herself to pull back. "What are we doing, Marc?"

He lifted his head from where he was licking a warm strip just below her neckline. "I would have thought that was obvious, Isa."

She blushed then, her face turning hot at the sardonic amusement in his tone and the powerful look in his eye. "I just mean…" She turned away, refusing to look at him. "I don't know what you want from me."

"Yes, you do." He straightened up then and looked her straight in the eye. Meeting his gaze when she felt so vulnerable, so uncertain, was one of the hardest things she'd ever done. But she forced herself to do it. Forced herself not to flinch or blink or look away. She had a right to know what she was getting into. With their history, this could be anything from revenge sex to reunion sex or a bunch of things in between.

Before she gave herself to him, she needed to know just what it was.

Except Marc had always been better at bedroom games

than she. More experienced, more able to control his responses. More able to articulate his thoughts and wishes. Tonight was no different.

"I want you, Isa," he told her, his hands stroking up and down her back in a rhythm that was at once soothing and arousing. "I want to kiss your breasts, to take your nipples into my mouth and see if you can still come from just the feel of me rolling them against my tongue and teeth."

She gasped then, didn't even try to hide the flush of arousal his words sent ricocheting through her.

"I want to be on my knees in front of you. I want to lick along your sex and feel you come on my tongue."

His words were so powerful, the need in his voice so seductive, that she grew wet from them alone.

"I want to pick you up and press you against the nearest wall. Want to feel your gorgeous legs wrap around my waist as I slide into you, nice and slow. I want to feel you clench around me, want to hear you call my name."

"Marc." She cried out his name and it was as much a demand as a plea. "I need—"

"I want you to come again and again and again. On my fingers, on my dick, on my tongue. Until all you know is pleasure. Until—"

He broke off as she threaded her hands into his hair and pulled his mouth to hers in a kiss so hard she knew her lips would be bruised. Not that she cared. Right now, all she cared about was Marc and this moment and the feel of him inside her. She wanted to hold him, wanted him to empty himself inside her until she finally felt full.

Until she finally felt whole.

And then she wanted him to do it all again.

"Yes." She breathed the word into his mouth even as she ripped at the fine silk of his shirt, desperate to get it

off him. Desperate to feel his skin—hot and smooth—
against her own.

Marc growled low in his throat—whether at her acquiescence or the feel of her nails scratching against his chest,
she didn't know. Buttons flew and he shrugged out of his
ruined shirt even as he whipped her tank top over her head.

"You're so goddamn beautiful," he growled. And then
he was cupping her breasts in his calloused hands. She
jerked, arching into the sensation that was somehow familiar and brand-new at the same time.

It was a double shot of sensation, to both watch and feel
as he touched her. Need—hot and powerful—skyrock-
eted inside her with each swirl of his fingers around her
nipples. It raced through her blood, slid from nerve ending to nerve ending until she burned with it, consumed by
it. Until all she could think or feel, all she could smell or
taste or see, was him.

Finally—finally—his thumbs brushed fully over her
nipples and she cried out at the streak of pleasure that shot
through her. She clutched at his shoulders. Arched her
back. And offered herself to him in a way she'd offered
herself to no other man.

In answer, he dropped to his knees in front of her.
Pulled her yoga pants and panties down her legs. Pressed
wet, openmouthed kisses to her belly, her rib cage, her
breasts. And then, when she was whimpering—when her
hands were clutching at his hair and her body was trembling with the need to feel him—he took her nipple in his
mouth and sucked hard enough to make her scream.

He did it again and again, lashing his tongue back and
forth over the hard bud until she trembled on the brink
of orgasm. She fought it, not wanting to give in to him
so easily. And not, she admitted in the deepest parts of
herself, wanting it to end so quickly. It had been too long

since Marc had held her, kissed her, made love to her, and if this was her one shot to have him again, she wasn't going to rush it.

But then he pinched her other nipple between his thumb and middle finger—all while he continued to suck and lick and bite at her other nipple. Her knees went weak and she clutched onto his shoulders for support, her hips moving restlessly against his chest as she drew closer and closer to the edge.

As if sensing her dilemma, Marc pulled his mouth away from her breast. She whimpered—actually whimpered—until he fiercely whispered, "Let go, Isa. It's okay. I've got you. I promise, I've got you, baby."

And then his mouth was back on her breast and she lost it completely. Dark and broken sounds fell from her lips as she spiraled up, up, up, up.

"Yes, baby," Marc encouraged, his fingers pinching her nipple a little more tightly. She cried out, scratching her nails down his back.

She was right there, her body poised to fly over the edge. Right there, right there, right—Marc bit her, gently, and with a scream that she was sure her neighbors could hear, she hurtled straight into ecstasy, her body convulsing again and again.

He held her, using his mouth and hands to draw out her pleasure until she was an incoherent mess. Then he pulled her close, wrapped his arms around her and murmured sweet love words against her damp skin.

She didn't understand what was happening here, didn't know what had transformed the angry man from earlier into the tender lover she remembered, but she wasn't going to worry about it. Not now, when her body was still singing with the most powerful orgasm she'd had in six years. Not now, when she was wrapped up in his arms so tightly that she could feel his heart beating against her skin. Not now, when she felt whole for the first time since Marc had kicked her out.

She'd do well to remember that—he'd kicked her out with nothing but the clothes on her back. And she would remember it. She *would*. Later. Right now, when she was naked and vulnerable and sated, she wanted to hold him and be held by him.

Wanted to love him and be loved by him—even if it was only her body she dared to give him. Even if it was only his body she was getting in return. Well, his body and long moments of completely unimaginable pleasure.

It wasn't enough, wasn't close to enough, but if it was all she would ever have of him, she would take it.

Six years ago, she'd learned that the future would come whether she worried about it or not. So here, now, she wouldn't worry about what came next. She would have this night, have Marc, and for once, let the future take care of itself.

Six

God, he'd missed her. Missed the taste of her skin. Missed the feel of her body against his. Missed the sound of her cries—broken and breathless—as she came for him. Even as he held her, even as he throbbed with the need for relief, he wanted to hear those sounds again. It wasn't an admission that came easy to him, not with everything that lay between them. But it was the truth, one he'd tried to ignore for six long years.

One—like her—he was desperate to get out of his system, once and for all.

Pushing to his feet, he picked Isa up and held her against his chest. "Which way is your bedroom?"

She stared up at him with passion-dazed eyes, and even though he felt as though he would die if he didn't get inside her in the next two minutes, he couldn't help lowering his head and, once again, taking her mouth with his.

She responded to him like she always did—with warmth

and fire and sweet, sweet surrender. He continued to kiss her as he headed down the hall, continued to kiss her as he lay her across the queen-size bed with the sexy red comforter. Continued to kiss her as he stripped down to the skin. And then he climbed onto the bed next to her and worshipped her the way he used to. The way he'd longed to for so, so long—with his hands and mouth and body touching, teasing, tasting every inch of her soft, sweet-smelling skin.

Isa moaned, her hands clutching at his hair, her body arching beneath him. His own need was sharp and violent inside him, but he wanted to see her come again. Wanted to steep himself in the sound and scent and feel of her as he gave her as much pleasure as she could take.

Fastening his mouth on her neck, he sucked a bruise into the sensitive skin. She shuddered, crying out his name as her fingernails raked down his back.

The quick, sharp pain loosed some wild thing in him he didn't even know was buried there. His control slipped the iron grip he'd kept on it from the moment she'd let him kiss her on that balcony.

And then his lips and tongue skimmed over her torso, her breasts, her stomach, her hips, her sex. He wanted to explore all of her, needed to find each and every change to her body that the past six years had wrought. The extra-fullness of her breasts, the new freckles on the soft insides of her elbows, the three small scars near her belly button that weren't there the last time he'd made love to her.

He traced his fingers over them, started to ask what had happened. But it wasn't his business—*she* wasn't his business—anymore, and he'd do well to remember that.

Except the words escaped of their own volition. "What happened here?"

"What? Where?" Her voice was husky, dazed with plea-

sure. Pleasure he had given her, he thought with grim satisfaction. Not that pansy-ass professor who couldn't keep
his hands off her at the cocktail party.

"Here." He ran a finger over the scars again.

"Oh." She sighed, her fingers sliding down his chest
to toy with his nipples as she answered, "Emergency ap-
pendectomy."

Her answer floated past him and pleasure coursed
through him as she played with him. Her fingers squeezed
and stroked and pinched as she pressed hot kisses to his
neck and shoulders and chest.

"Isa." It was a warning, more a growl than an actual
word.

She didn't pay any attention, though. Instead, she slid
slowly down the bed as her mouth worked its way over
his pecs, his stomach, his abdomen. He was still above
her, but that fact wasn't hampering her at all as her mouth
trailed hot kisses over the sparse trail of hair that led from
his belly button.

And then she took him in her mouth, sucking him deep
even as her tongue licked hotly against the length of him.
He bit off a curse, taking her ministrations for several
long seconds, his arms trembling as they supported his
weight above her.

But when she pulled him deep and he felt his release
gathering at the base of his spine, he pulled away with a
groan.

"What?" she asked, eyes dazed and mouth swollen as
she reached for him. "I want to—"

"I want to be inside you when I come," he told her. He
didn't know why it mattered—pleasure was pleasure, after
all—but it did. He wanted the first time he came with Isa
after their long separation to be when he was inside her.

Ignoring her moan of protest, he shifted off her for several long seconds as he retrieved his pants from the floor. He grabbed his wallet, pulled out a condom. Seconds later, he was back on the bed, his body covering hers.

Sliding a hand between her thighs to make sure she was ready for him, he relished the wet heat that told him she was as affected by him as he was by her.

"Marc, please," she gasped, her hands sliding around to pull him more firmly against her.

"I'm right here, baby." The endearment slipped out, as did the soft kisses he pressed to her flushed cheeks.

And then he was sliding inside her, sliding *home*, after far too long. Isa gasped, moaned, her body arching beneath his. Her arms wrapping around his shoulders. Her legs twining around his hips.

God, she felt good. Warm, wet, willing. *Amazing.*

He plunged into her again and again, relishing the way her body rose to meet his.

The way she whimpered.

The way her beautiful, dark eyes turned hazy as she got closer and closer to orgasm.

He was close, too—so close that it was an agony not to come. But he wanted—needed—her to come first. He wanted to see her face as pleasure took her, wanted to feel her body clutching him, holding him deep inside.

Sweat rolled down his muscles, pulled at the small of his back as he continued to build the pleasure—and the tension—between them. Isa moaned, her voice low and broken as she pleaded with him to send her over. Pleaded with him to let her come.

And while there was nothing he wanted more than to give her release—and take his own—he also wasn't ready to let her go. Wasn't ready for this to end. It had been so long since he'd held Isa like this, that he wanted to make every second last forever. Who knew when—or if—they'd ever have this chance again.

Except Isa wouldn't let him wait. Clutching at him with her arms and legs and body, she pulled him close. Pressed hot kisses to his mouth and jaw and neck. Sucked a bruise of her own right above his collarbone.

It was that mark, that brand, that sent him over the edge. Slipping a hand between them, he stroked her once, twice.

That was all it took to have her crying out his name as her body clenched rhythmically around him. And then he let go, too, coming deep inside her as pleasure roared through him like a freight train. Coming until he couldn't figure out where she left off and he began…or how he was going to live without this, without her.

He woke up feeling better than he had in years. Six years to be exact. His body was sated, his mind at peace. It was a strange feeling—so strange that it sent Marc hurtling from sleep into wakefulness with a speed that was practically painful.

His eyes flew open, and as he glimpsed Isa's bright red hair fanned out next to him on the pillow, the events of the previous night came flooding back in graphic, and arousing, detail. As his body responded to the private slide show in his head he thought about rolling over. About pulling her on top of him. About sliding into her as those gorgeous brown eyes of hers blinked open.

He wanted that, wanted her—even after all the times he'd had her the night before—with an intensity that bordered on desperation. Which was why he did exactly the opposite.

Rolling out of bed, he grabbed his pants and padded quietly down the hall to her kitchen, which was the last place he remembered having his shirt. Sure enough, it was crumpled on the ground, along with his shoes.

As he pulled his clothes back on, he tried not to think about the night before. Tried not to think about how good it had felt to have Isa back in his arms.

He'd never felt with another woman what he felt when he was with her. When they'd been together—when he'd loved and trusted her—making love to her had been an amazing high. He had lost himself in her day after day, night after night. It probably should have been scary to a guy like him—who had trouble trusting anyone—but it hadn't been. He'd been so crazy about her that he had never imagined she might betray him.

But she had and now they were here. The only problem was, he didn't know where here was any more than he knew where he wanted it to be. Yes, last night the sex had been fantastic. More than fantastic, it had been hot and exciting.

But it wasn't the pleasure that had him awake as dawn slowly streaked its rainbow fingers across the ocean outside her window. No, it wasn't the pleasure that was freaking him out. It was the way his body and mind felt balanced and rested and replete for the first time in a very long time.

He didn't like the fact that Isa was responsible for the feeling. It had been less than twenty-four hours since he'd walked into the back of her classroom and seen her teaching and already they were back in bed. Already he was thinking about taking her again. Already, he was thinking of taking her back.

And that was where the trouble lay. Because there was no way he could do that. No way he could forget that she'd betrayed him six years ago. No way he could forget that she had chosen her father—a man who had stolen from Marc,

who had destroyed years of his work, who had nearly ruined everything he'd worked for—over him.

Because if she could do it once, in the middle of the
most intense and powerful love affair he'd ever had, then
she could do it again. And if that was the case, then he
needed to walk away right now. Before he fell victim to
all the little things he'd once loved about her.

Like her smile and her scent.

Like her wicked sense of humor and her even more
wicked intellect.

Like how sleepy she was in the morning, when she
wrapped herself around him and begged for kisses.

"You're still here." Her voice was husky with sleep, but
when he turned to face her, her eyes were wide-awake. "I
thought you'd left."

"Not yet. But I do need to get going. I've got to get to
the office."

"It's Saturday."

"I'm aware of that. But I work on Saturdays." He pretty
much worked every day. "Especially now that I've taken
on the class at the institute."

He thought about crossing to her, about dropping a kiss
on her still-swollen lips. But if he was honest with himself, he was as uneasy as she obviously was. More unsure
of what he wanted to do and how he wanted to do it than
he'd ever been in his life. It was an uncomfortable feeling,
one he didn't like at all.

"You never used to work on Saturdays." Her voice was
even, but still it sounded like an accusation. Which, in
turn, made him feel guilty, even though he had nothing
to feel guilty for.

He lashed out before he could think better of it. "Yeah,
well, six years ago I thought I was safe. I thought I'd built
the company up to a place where I could breathe a little,

where I could take an occasional day off and trust things would be okay. If you remember correctly, that didn't work out too well for me." He didn't even try to keep the temper out of his voice. How dare she accuse him of running out on her when she'd been the one to betray him? The one to disappear off the face of the earth for more than half a decade?

She winced, but kept her gaze steady on his as she said, "How long are you going to keep throwing that in my face?"

The small licks of anger grew into wilder flames. "I've mentioned it twice in the last twenty-four hours," he told her, forcing his voice to remain steady. "And before that, I hadn't talked to you in six damn years. So tell me, please, how is it, exactly, that I'm throwing the past in your face?"

"I don't know. But it feels like you are." She wrapped her arms around her waist, hugging herself in a gesture that screamed discomfort and defensiveness.

It should have given him pause, *would* have given him pause if he wasn't so uncomfortable and defensive himself. "Maybe that's your guilty conscience talking. Maybe there's a part of you that feels like you deserve whatever you think I'm doing to you."

"Maybe I do. But that doesn't mean I'm reading the situation wrong." She paused and took a deep breath as if she was gathering her courage.

All of a sudden, he felt ashamed. He hadn't come here to berate her, to make her nervous in her own home. "Say it, Isa. Whatever it is you want to say, just get it off your chest."

"All right." She licked her lips in a gesture that was as familiar to him as her skin sliding against his own. "It's just, I can't figure out what last night was about."

"I'm not sure what you mean." A sick feeling stirred

deep inside him. He didn't want to think too closely about his rationale for last night. At least not beyond scratching an itch that had been six long years in the making.

"I mean, what was the point of it? Was it your way of getting revenge after all this time? Of trying to hurt me?" Despite her earlier nervousness, she said the words as if they were no big deal. As if she'd anticipated he'd do something like that all along.

It got to him, in a huge way. Because last night had been about a lot of things—lust, confusion, jealousy, need—but he could honestly say that revenge had never entered into it. Not when he went out to speak with her on the balcony. Not when he made the decision to follow her home. And definitely not when he showed up at her door. Not once had he been thinking of revenge. Maybe he should have been, but he hadn't. Instead, he'd been thinking about her. Just her.

The fact that she obviously hadn't felt the same way... that she had been analyzing his motives—and him—from the moment she opened her door, wounded him. No, that wasn't true. It didn't hurt him. It made him feel like a fool, and that made him furious. She'd already played him once, and he'd be damned if he ever let her do that to him again. He wasn't that stupid.

"I wouldn't call it revenge so much as closure," he finally told her after several long seconds of silence. "Our relationship ended so abruptly that it always felt...unfinished. I didn't like it."

"And now?" she asked, face calm and brow raised inquiringly.

"Now? It feels done."

It was a lie, but she didn't have to know that. And it wasn't as if it would be a lie forever. This was exactly the closure he'd needed, he assured himself as he bent over and retrieved his keys from where they'd fallen on the floor. He knew she was okay, knew she hadn't been harmed by the cruel way he'd had her removed from his apartment all those years ago. And he'd been able to touch her after all this time, to slake a thirst he hadn't known was there until he'd seen her yesterday. That was enough. More than enough.

Or, at least, it would be.

His will was iron strong and he would make it the truth if it killed him. He'd spent too many years of his life thinking, worrying, *caring* about a woman who would never do the same for him.

That ended here. Now. He knew Isa was safe. He'd even had one last night with her. It was more than enough. It was time for him to close this chapter of his life and move on, once and for all. And he would start by walking out Isa's door.

"Thanks for last night," he told her, dropping a kiss on her cheek as he headed for the entryway. "It was fun."

She nodded, but didn't say anything as he opened the door, stepped onto her porch and took her front steps two at a time. She still didn't say anything, even as he made his way down the walkway to his car.

He didn't know what he wanted her to say—didn't know what he wanted from her at all. But as the front door closed quietly behind him, he knew that silence wasn't it. He knew he wanted more from her than that.

But then, he always had. She'd just never been able to give it.

She was an idiot.

After closing—and locking—the front door after Marc, Isa turned and marched straight back to the master bedroom. Though there was a part of her that wanted nothing

more than to fling herself onto the mattress and pull the
covers over her head, she knew that wasn't going to work.
Partly because her problems would still be there, waiting
for her, when she finally managed to resurface. And partly
because the sheets still smelled like Marc and she wasn't
masochistic enough to climb into them again. Not when
she could barely breathe without memories of what had
happened last night slicing through her like broken glass.

She'd known while she was doing it that she was making a mistake. After all, Marc wasn't one to forgive betrayal easily. And yet she'd done it anyway. She'd fallen
into bed with him. Had given herself to him over and
over again without worrying about consequences. Or what
would happen in the morning. Or whether or not he was
just using her. Instead, for a little while, she'd allowed
herself to believe that miracles could happen. She'd allowed herself to believe that it could be like it was six
years ago, before her father had ruined everything. Before she'd let him.

Suddenly, she couldn't stand the sight of the rum-
pled bed for one second more. She threw herself at it in a
frenzy, stripping the sheets, the blankets, even the mattress
pad. When she was done—when the bed was completely
empty—she carried it all into her doll-sized laundry room
and shoved as much as she could fit into her washing machine. It would take two loads, but she didn't care. All that
mattered was getting rid of every last reminder of Marc
and the mistake she had made.

Then, once the bed was taken care of, she started on
herself. And realized erasing Marc from her body's memory was going to be a million times more difficult. After
all, memories of his existence, his touch, his smell, had
lived right under her skin for six long years, just waiting to spring back to life. And now that they had, she

wasn't sure she had the strength to banish them—to banish him—again.

Stripping off her nightgown, which had somehow absorbed the scent of him despite the fact that they'd slept naked, she dropped it into the pile of bedding that was still waiting to be washed. And then she walked, naked, down the hall and into the bedroom to take a shower.

As she waited for the water to get warm, she made the mistake of looking in the mirror. What she saw there nearly brought her to her knees.

She looked…like she'd spent the night getting ravaged. Her hair was wild; her skin flushed a rosy pink wherever his stubble had touched her. Her mouth was swollen; her eyes dreamy and a little unfocused. And there were bruises. On her throat. On the outer side of her left breast. On her right hip. On the delicate skin of her inner thigh. They were love bites. Hickeys. Small reminders of him sucked into her skin.

As if she needed the reminders. As if she could forget what he'd done to her—what they'd done to each other.

But she *needed* to forget, she told herself fiercely. She needed to bury the memories of last night somewhere deep inside so she wouldn't have to think about them every time she walked into her bedroom. Or every time she saw him at the institute. She'd spent six long years hearing his name—her specialty was conflict diamonds, after all, and his company was the biggest conflict-free diamond source in North America—which meant his name came up a lot in her research, her lectures, her papers.

She'd managed to ignore it for a long time, to put distance between what had happened between them and the businessman who was making so many important and exciting decisions in the field. Now that she'd slept with him again, she would have to go back to how it had been in the old days. Ignoring every mention of him, writing her way around him, pretending he didn't exist. Not forever, mind you, but for a little while. Just until she could get her head on straight. Just until she could breathe again without bleeding inside.

Fake it until you make it, she told herself grimly as she stepped into the shower and scrubbed herself raw in an attempt to erase the memory of his touch from her skin. Wasn't that the phrase? She'd spent a long time pretending that year in Manhattan had never happened and had finally gotten to a place where she was happy. Healthy. And now, here he was, back again, shaking everything up. Shaking her up. And she was just supposed to go along for the ride.

Cold, hot, cold, hot. Cold.

No. Not this time. And never again. He was too dominant, his moods too mercurial, and she wasn't going to take the ride with him again. It had been fun once, but that was before she'd had anything to lose but him. She'd been drifting when she met him at that gala all those years ago. Stealing had lost its thrill and she'd had nothing to replace it until him.

That wasn't the case anymore. Now she had a career. She had friendships. She had a *life*. And she'd worked too damn hard for that life to let him come in and turn it topsy-turvy because of old mistakes. And even older chemistry.

No, from now on she would ignore Marc whenever she saw him. A quick nod of acknowledgment if she couldn't get around it, but that was it. No interaction, no arguing, and for God's sake, definitely no sex.

Because any interaction with Marc would lead to questions from her peers that she couldn't answer. Questions that would bring up a past she couldn't talk about.

Because one of the world's leading experts on diamonds—a woman who was allowed into and left alone in vaults all over the world—couldn't also be the daughter of the most successful jewel thief who'd ever lived. It didn't work that way.

And since all she'd had was her work from the moment Marc cast her out on that dirty New York sidewalk, since it was what had saved her when the rest of her world had imploded, there was no way she was risking her career for him. Not now. Not ever again. No matter how powerful the chemistry or how good the sex.

Some things just weren't meant to be. And her relationship with Marc was obviously one of those things.

Now all she had to do was remember that.

Seven

"We have a problem."

Marc looked up as Nic blew right past Marc's assistant and entered his office without so much as a knock—or a hello. "What's going on?"

His brother slammed his hand down on the desk hard enough to rattle everything resting on top of it—including Marc's laptop and cup of coffee. For expediency's sake—and to give him a second to settle the alarm raking through his stomach—Marc grabbed the coffee and put it on the credenza behind him.

When he turned back to face Nic, Marc was completely composed. He had a feeling he would need it, since Nic was not one to fly off the handle over every small thing. He was volatile, sure—the flip side of the charm that made him such a perfect fit for the public side of the company—but he never panicked. But Marc was pretty sure that panic was what he saw in Nic's eyes right now. And he'd be lying if he said it didn't make him more than a little nervous.

"Tell me."

"I just got off the phone with a reporter from the *LA Times*. She's doing an exposé on Bijoux and wanted a comment before the article goes to print."

"An exposé? What the hell does she have to expose?" Marc stood up then, walked around the desk. "Between you and me, we're in charge of every aspect of this company. Nothing happens here that we don't know about."

"That's exactly what I told her."

"And?" He ground out the words. "What's she exposing?"

"According to her, the fact that we're pulling diamonds from conflict areas, certifying them as conflict free, and then passing them onto the consumer at the higher rate in order to maximize our profits."

"That's ridiculous."

"I know it's ridiculous! I told her as much. She says she has an unimpeachable source."

"Who's the source?"

Nic thrust a frustrated hand through his hair. "She wouldn't tell me that."

"Of course she wouldn't tell you that, because the source is bullshit. The whole story is bullshit. I know where every single shipment of diamonds comes from. I personally inspect every mine on a regular basis. The certification numbers come straight to me and only our in-house diamond experts—experts that I have handpicked and trust implicitly—ever get near those numbers."

"I told her all of that. I invited her to come in and take a tour of our new facilities and see exactly how things work here at Bijoux."

"And what did she say?"

"She said she had tried to come for a tour, but PR had put her off. It's too late now. The story is slotted to run on

Friday and that she really would like a comment from us before it goes to print."

"That's in six days."

"I'm aware of that. It's why I'm here, freaking out."

"Screw that." Marc picked up his phone and dialed an in-house number. Waited impatiently for the line to be picked up.

"Hollister Banks."

"Hollister. This is Marc. I need you in my office now."

"Be there in five."

He didn't bother to say goodbye before hanging up and dialing another number. "Lisa Brown, how may I help you?"

He told his top diamond inspector the same thing he'd just told the head of his legal team.

"But, Marc, I just got in a whole new shipment—"

"So put it in the vault and then get up here." He must have sounded as impatient as he felt, because she didn't argue with him again. She just agreed before quietly hanging up the phone.

It took Lisa and Hollister less than three minutes to get to Marc's office, and soon the four of them were gathered in the small sitting area to the left of his desk, listening as Nic once again recounted his discussion with the reporter.

"Who's the source?" Marc demanded of Lisa as soon as Nic finished up.

"Why are you asking me? I have no idea who would make up a false story like this and feed it to the *LA Times*. I'm sure it's none of our people."

"The reporter seemed pretty adamant that it was an insider. Someone who had the position and the access to prove what he or she is saying."

"But that's impossible. Because what the person is saying isn't *true*. The claims are preposterous," Lisa asserted.

"Marc and I are the first and last in the chain of command when it comes to accepting and certifying the conflict-free diamonds. There's no way one of us would make a mistake like that—and we sure as hell wouldn't lie about the gems being conflict-free to make extra money. So even if someone messed with the diamonds between when I see them and when Marc does, he would catch it."

"Not to mention the fact that there are cameras everywhere, manned twenty-four seven by security guards who get paid very well to make sure no one tampers with our stones," Nic added.

"What this person is saying just isn't possible," Lisa continued. "That's why Marc insists on being the last point of contact for the stones before we ship them out. He verifies the geology and the ID numbers associated with them."

"There is a way it would work," Marc interrupted, his stomach churning sickly. "If I were involved in the duplicity, it would explain everything."

"But you're not!" Nic said at the same time Lisa exclaimed, "That's absurd!"

Their faith in him was the only bright point in a day that was rapidly going from awful to worse.

"It's what they'll argue," Hollister said, and though it was obvious by his tone that he disagreed, the thought still stung. This was more than a company to Marc, more than cold stones and colder cash. His great-grandfather had started the company nearly a hundred years before and it had been run by a Durand ever since. He'd put his life into continuing that tradition and building Bijoux into the second largest diamond distributor in the world. He'd brought it into the twenty-first century and created a business model that didn't exploit the people who most needed protection. Not dealing in blood diamonds was a matter of honor for him. To be accused of doing that which he most abhorred…it made him furious—and determined.

"I don't care what you have to do," he told Hollister. "I want that story stopped. We've worked too hard to build this company into what it is to have another setback—especially one like this. The jewel theft six years ago hurt our reputation and nearly bankrupted us. This will destroy everything Nic and I have been trying to do. You know as well as I, even if we prove the accusations false in court, the stigma will still be attached. Even if we get the *LA Times* to print a retraction, it won't matter. The damage will have already been done. I'm not having it. Not this time. Not about something like this."

It took every ounce of his self-control not to plow his fist into the wall. Goddamn it. He wasn't doing this again. "Call the editor of the *LA Times*. Tell him the story is blatant bullshit and if he runs it I will sue their asses and tie them up in court for years to come. By the time I'm done, they won't have a computer to their name let alone a press to run the paper on."

"I'll do my best, but—"

"Do better than your best. Do whatever it takes to make it happen. If you have to, remind them that they can't afford to go against Bijoux in today's precarious print media market. If they think they're going to do billions of dollars of damage to this company with a blatantly false story based on a source they won't reveal, and that I won't retaliate, then they are bigger fools than I'm already giving them credit for. You can assure them that if they don't provide me with definitive proof as to the truth of their claims, then I will make it my life's work to destroy everyone and everything involved in this story. And when you tell them that, make sure they understand I don't make idle threats."

"I'll lay it out for them. But, Marc," Hollister cautioned,

"if you're wrong and you've antagonized the largest newspaper on the West Coast—"

"I'm not wrong. We don't deal in blood diamonds. We will never deal in blood diamonds and anyone who says differently is a goddamn liar."

"We need to do more than threaten them," Nic said into the silence that followed his pronouncements. "We need to prove to them that they're wrong."

"And how exactly are we going to do that?" Lisa asked. "If we don't know who they're getting information from, or even what that information is, how can we contradict them?"

"By hiring an expert in conflict diamonds," Hollister chimed in. "By taking him up to Canada where we get our stock, letting him examine the mines we pull from. And then bringing him back here and giving him access to anything and everything he wants. We don't have any secrets—at least not of the blood diamond variety. So let's prove that."

"Yes, but getting an expert of that caliber on board could take weeks," Lisa protested. "There are barely a dozen people in the world with the credentials to sign off unquestioningly on our diamonds. Even if we pay twice the going rate, there's no guarantee that one of them will be available."

"But one is available," Nic told her even as he cast a wary look at Marc. "She lives right here in San Diego and teaches at GIA. She could totally do it."

Hell. He couldn't say he was surprised—from the moment Hollister had suggested hiring an expert, Marc had known they would end up here. But that didn't make it any easier to take.

"Dude, you look like you swallowed a bug," his brother told him.

Yeah, that was pretty much how he felt, too, except worse. Because, no. He wasn't calling her. He *couldn't* call her. Not with their distant past and definitely not with what had just happened between them the night before. She'd laugh in his face. And if she didn't…if she didn't, she'd probably deliberately sabotage them. No, he wouldn't put the future of his company in her hands.

He said as much to Nic, who rolled his eyes in exasperation. "Weren't you the one saying we can't afford to screw around with this? Isa's here, she has the experience, and if you pay her well and get a sub to carry her classes, she's probably available. It doesn't get much better than that."

"You should give her a call," Hollister urged.

"Yeah, absolutely," agreed Lisa. "I'd forgotten about Isabella Moreno being here in San Diego. I've met her a few times and she's really lovely—we should totally get her. I can try to talk to her, if you'd like."

Marc almost said yes, almost passed the buck onto Lisa to deal with. But he couldn't. It would be a slap in the face to Isa—an even bigger one than he'd already delivered to her this morning—and he couldn't afford that. Couldn't afford to antagonize her when she might very well be the only thing standing between Bijoux and total ruin.

The irony of the situation was not lost on him.

"No," he told Lisa harshly, after a few uncomfortable seconds passed. "I'll take care of getting her on board."

He sounded more confident than he felt. Then again, it wasn't as if he had a choice. He couldn't fail. Not now, not on this. His family's business depended on it.

He would do whatever it took to convince Isa to take on Bijoux—and him.

Eight

Isa was in the middle of a cleaning frenzy, one that involved scrubbing down every surface in her house that Marc might have touched. She knew it was ridiculous, knew it had to be her mind playing tricks on her, but that didn't matter. Not when she could smell him everywhere.

Inconsiderate bastard, leaving his dark honey and pine scent all over her house. She refused to acknowledge the little voice that whispered it wasn't her house he'd left his scent on. It was her.

She'd made it through the entire space and was on her knees scrubbing the bottom shelf of her refrigerator when the doorbell rang. She nearly ignored it—it wasn't like she was in the mood to talk to anyone. But when the ringing gave way to a loud and urgent pounding, she rushed to the front door and pulled it open. She lived in a good neighborhood, but that didn't mean someone wasn't in trouble. Maybe they needed—

She froze as she looked straight up and into Marc's narrowed eyes.

So not an emergency, then.

She slammed the door shut in his face before she could worry about what she was giving away by doing so. Then she sagged against it and forced herself to pull air into lungs that had forgotten how to breathe.

What was he doing here? When he'd walked out this morning, she'd been certain she'd never have to see him again—maybe only from a distance on the GIA campus. Had counted on it, in fact. No matter what she'd told herself, her feelings for him, for what had happened last night, were still too raw for her to face him again.

Not yet, she told herself as she worked to get her ragged heartbeat under control. Preferably not ever, but definitely not yet.

Except Marc hadn't gotten the message. The pounding on her door started again, along with his voice, low and urgent, ordering her to "Open up, Isabelle."

It was his use of her formal first name that got her brain functioning again.

She thought about ignoring him. About walking into her bedroom at the back of the house and turning on music, the TV, the shower—anything to drown out the sound of his voice. But doing so would make her look even more ridiculous, more pathetic, than she already did. And that was saying something.

It was that thought—along with her smarting pride—that finally made the decision for her. She rubbed her suddenly sweaty palms down the front of her jean-clad thighs and turned to open the door.

"Hi, Marc," she said as she once again peered up at him, a fake—but bright—smile curving her lips upward. "Sorry about that. You caught me in the middle of something…" She tried to ignore the way her voice trailed off uncertainly, prayed that he would be gentleman enough to do the same. She didn't know what it was about Marc Durand that turned her into a babbling schoolgirl with a crush on the most popular boy in school, but she didn't like it.

Marc must have been feeling merciful, because he didn't call her on her blatant lie. Nor did he try to put his hands on her. Instead, he raised a brow and asked, "Can I come in?"

No. She had spent the past two hours eradicating his presence from her house and now he wanted back in? With his gorgeous scent and his larger-than-life personality and his big hands, which he had used to drive her to orgasm again and again?

No, he couldn't come in. He shouldn't come in.

But, big surprise, knowing the danger was very different from acting on it. Instead of sending him away with another slammed door in his face, she pulled the door open wider and stepped back so he could get inside without his body brushing against her traitorous one. "Of course, yes. I assume you're here for your socks?"

Both brows went up this time. "My socks?"

"Yes." She cleared her throat, awkwardly. "They're very nice socks. I found them when I was straightening up. You must have forgotten them when you left this morning."

Very nice socks? Was she suddenly twelve? she asked herself fiercely. Socks were socks, for God's sake.

Judging by the strange look he shot her, Marc definitely seemed to think so, too. "Oh, um, thanks? I hadn't really noticed."

"How do you not notice that you're not wearing socks with your dress shoes?" She glanced down at his bare ankles doubtfully, even as she told herself to forget about the damn socks. "I can't believe your shoes are all that comfortable, even if they are Hugo Boss."

Then she bit her lip because, really, could she sound more obsessed? She kept harping about his "nice socks" *and* she knew what kind of dress shoes the man wore. He was probably counting himself lucky for the narrow escape he'd made this morning.

But he didn't seem to be inching away in alarm, any more than he seemed concerned by her intimate knowledge of his footwear. Instead he simply said, "I've had other, more important things on my mind today."

For one heart-stopping moment, she thought he was talking about her. About *them*. Her stomach jumped with excitement, even as her brain quelled the reaction. Despite her rather asinine reactions since he'd come to the door, she didn't want him, she reminded herself firmly. And he couldn't possibly want her. Not after all the ugliness that had passed between them—both six years ago and again this morning.

With that thought front and foremost in her mind, she cleared the last of the weirdness away and demanded, "So what are you doing here, then? I don't have much time to stand around and talk—I've got a date in a couple hours and I have to get ready."

"You have a *date*." He said the words in a flat, emotionless tone that she might have mistaken for disbelief, and lack of concern, if she hadn't seen the spark of anger in the depths of his eyes.

"I do." It was really more of an afternoon cocktail party to celebrate the opening of a prestigious jewelry collection by one of her former students at a local gallery, but she wasn't going to tell Marc that. Not when that event was the only thing standing between her and the utter humiliation that came with reliving the morning, when Marc had walked away from her without a backward glance.

"I do."

"With that professor from yesterday?" His voice was a growl now, his eyes a few shades darker than normal. And suddenly he was walking deeper into the house, each step causing her to retreat a little more until her back was, literally, against the wall and he was standing right there, his powerful body pressing into her as he looked down at her, his eyes hot and his mouth twisted in a displeased snarl.

There was a part of her that wanted to give in to his obvious dominance, but that part didn't get to be in control. So she tilted her chin up and met him glare for glare. "How is who I go out with any of your business?"

"Oh, it's my business," he growled as his hand came up to bracket her throat, his fingers resting on her collarbone while his thumb rubbed gently against the love bite he'd sucked into her throat sometime last night. His hold wasn't painful, wasn't even threatening. Instead, it was possessive, arousing as hell, though she fought to keep from acknowledging that fact.

"It isn't," she assured him.

"It is." His fingers massaged her collarbone before sliding slowly up her neck to her cheek. "I was the one inside you just a few hours ago. The one making you come. The one making you *scream*."

She melted at his words, her lower body going hot and wet at the snarly, desire-filled sound of his voice. But still she held her ground, refusing to let him know how much he affected her. "Maybe. But you were also the one babbling about closure and hightailing it out the door this morning as fast as your feet could carry you."

He wrapped his other hand around her waist. "I don't babble."

"And I don't beg," she told him firmly.

"You begged me last night." He stepped even closer,

dropping his head so that his lips were barely an inch from hers.

She felt her muscles go weak, felt herself sag against him for one precious second. Then two. Then three. His hand curved around the back of her head, his fingers tangling in her hair, and she almost gave in. Almost gave herself up to him again. It's what her body wanted—more of the insidious pleasure he could bring her with just a touch of his fingers, his lips, his skin.

But then memories of what it had felt like when he'd kicked her out of his apartment all those years ago rose up inside her, mingled with the hurt from this morning that she'd tried so hard to deny all day.

She wasn't giving in, wasn't yielding to the sexual magnetism he wielded like a sorcerer.

Shoving at his chest, she squeezed out from between his body and the wall. "I'm pretty sure I'm not the only one who begged," she called over her shoulder as she walked down the hall to her kitchen, away from him.

She figured her comment would anger him—she had counted on it, as a matter of fact. But after a second of disgruntled silence, Marc tossed his head back and laughed. His reaction was a million times more disconcerting than what she'd expected. Partly because it was the first time she'd heard him laugh since he'd walked into her classroom the afternoon before and partly because it was a good laugh. A really good laugh, low and smoky and filled with a joy that told her it was genuine, despite the circumstances.

"Touché," he said as she got herself a glass of ice water and then drained it in two long gulps.

When the water was done—when she felt as if she had herself under control, at last—Isa turned back to him and demanded, "Why are you here, Marc? I'm pretty sure we said everything we needed to say to each other this morning before you left."

He winced slightly. "I know I was a little harsh—"

"Don't pull that smarmy rich boy routine on me!" she snapped. "You weren't harsh. You were definite. Sleeping with me was closure and once you'd done it you were finished, ready to move on." She tore her eyes away from his too-beautiful face to glance at the clock on the wall behind his head. "So try again. What do you really want?"

He stared at her for long seconds, until the heat between them grew intolerable. "You," he finally said. "I want you."

"Try again," she replied with a snort that in no way betrayed the riot of emotions exploding inside. "You've had me, twice. And both times it's ended with you kicking me to the curb."

"I didn't kick you to the curb this morning—"

"Maybe not literally, since this is my house," she told him with a shrug she hoped looked negligent. "But you definitely did it metaphorically. Which is fine, I get it. Closure, revenge, whatever. But that still doesn't explain why you're here now. What do you want from me?"

He paused, seeming to weigh his words as carefully as she'd been weighing hers.

Finally, just when she'd given up hope on him telling her anything, he ground out, "I need your help."

Nine

"My help?" She stared at him incredulously.

"Yes." He pulled back, putting some distance between them for the first time since he'd walked back into her house. Damn it. There was no way she would help him, not after what he'd just pulled.

He hadn't meant to go all possessive on her, hadn't meant to give in to the sensual need that throbbed between them with each breath they took. He was there because he needed her help professionally, not because he wanted to get her into bed again. Or at least, that was the lie he was telling himself.

Now that he'd given her some breathing room, she spun around. Pulled another glass out of the cabinet behind her. She filled it with ice and water before handing it to him and demanding, "Explain."

So he did, telling her about the article, about the damage it could do to Bijoux if it ran. About how they needed a conflict diamond expert to sign off on the fact that their stock was completely conflict free.

When he was done, she looked at him over the rim of her cup. "There are other experts out there. You could have gone to any of a dozen people and asked them to work for you."

"I could have, yes."

"But you came to me instead. Because you figured you could use our past to sway my results?"

Fury shot through him. "I don't need to sway your results. When you investigate Bijoux, you'll find that we use only responsibly sourced diamonds. I can assure you, there is not one blood diamond among our stock."

"That's a pretty big assurance," she told him. "How can you be sure?"

"Because I look at each and every diamond that comes through our place. I make sure that, geologically, they come from where we say they do."

"Every diamond?" she asked, skeptical. "You must clear ten thousand of them a month."

"More. And yes," he said before she could ask again, "I look at every single one."

"How do you have that kind of time? Don't you have a company to run?"

"I make time. I know that makes me a control freak, but I don't give a damn. My business almost died once because I took my eye off the ball. I can guarantee you that won't happen again."

She winced. Because of what he'd said or the angry way he'd said it, he didn't know. He should stop throwing that in her face, considering he needed her help, but she'd asked why he was the way he was about his business. What happened six years ago was a huge part of that.

She didn't say anything, didn't fire back like she normally would. That didn't reassure him, though. Not when she was looking at him with something akin to regret in her eyes. He wanted to believe it was for the past they shared, but his gut told him it was about his request.

Sure enough, after a long silence, she told him, "I can't do it."

"You mean you won't do it."

"No, I mean I *can't*. I've got a full load of classes this semester as well as a side project of my own going on—"

"This won't take long," he said. "A day and a half, two at the most for travel to Canada, then a couple days at my headquarters, comparing the mineral composition of my diamonds with those from the Canadian mines. Even if you wanted to trace a random sampling of serial numbers, shipments and documentation, it shouldn't take much longer than that."

"That's best-case scenario, if I don't find any irregularities."

"You won't," he assured her with total confidence. He knew his business inside out. There was no way conflict stones were going through Bijoux. No way. Not when he and Nic worked too damn hard to ensure that they always sourced responsibly.

"You can't guarantee that," she reiterated.

"I damn well can. My business is clean. My stones come from Canada and Australia and each and every one of them can be traced from the mine to me. There are no irregularities."

"You don't source from Africa at all? Or Russia?"

"No."

"There are a number of mines in both places that certify their diamonds as conflict free by Kimberley Process standards—"

"But I can't guarantee that no child labor went into

mining them. I can't know for sure where the profits are going. Most of the mines I use in Canada and Australia have shareholders that they answer to, and those that don't have very rigorous—and open—bookkeeping. My diamonds are as clean as I can possibly make them, Isa. Trust me on that."

She snorted a little, muttered something under her breath that sounded an awful lot like "Yeah, right."

He couldn't help stiffening at her response. She had no reason not to trust him—he'd never lied to her. He'd never betrayed her. He was the first to admit he'd acted like an ass when he'd had her removed from his building, but he hadn't schemed behind her back, hadn't lied over and over again because of misplaced loyalty. No, that had been her modus operandi.

He wanted to call her on it—any other time he *would* have called her on it—but right now, he needed her more than she needed him. The knowledge grated like hell. He'd sworn a long time ago never to give a woman power over him again and yet here he was, giving that power to not just any woman but to the one who had nearly destroyed him.

So instead of picking a fight he couldn't afford to lose, he swallowed back his bitterness and growled, "It's a short-term assignment but that doesn't mean it can't be very profitable for you. I know it's short notice, but I'm more than willing to double—or triple—your regular fee."

She reeled back as if he'd slapped her. "Are you trying to bribe me to certify your diamonds as conflict free?"

"*Bribe* you?" He went from annoyed to furious in two seconds flat. "I already explained that I have no reason to worry. The last thing I need to do is bribe someone to lie about my business."

"Then why the extra money? My regular fee is steep enough to make most companies wince."

"Jesus, you're suspicious."

"You have to admit, I have reason to be."

No, damn it, she didn't. He had never been anything but straight with her. "Bijoux isn't most companies. And I don't have the luxury of time. This ridiculous exposé is supposed to run on Friday and if I don't kill it, it's going to destroy my business. Why the hell wouldn't I pay double your regular fee if it meant you'd take the job?" This time he didn't bother to keep the bite out of his voice. Her lack of trust was getting to him, big-time, and he had no problem letting her know it.

Except Isa didn't seem to care. She narrowed her eyes at his tone, watching him for several long seconds. "You know this isn't going to work, right?" she finally said.

"It will. I've worked too hard to lose my company now."

"I don't mean the certification. I mean us working together. You need to find someone else."

"There is no one else, not with this short notice."

"Have you called around, tried to check it out?"

"No."

"Then how do you know that no one else is available? Stephen Vardeaux operates out of New York now and Byron M—"

"I don't want someone else," he snapped. "I want you."

"Why?" she asked suspiciously, her voice louder than usual with the same frustration that was rushing through him. "Because you think you can use our past to influence—"

"Goddamn it!" He roared as he finally lost his grip on his temper. "What have I ever done to make you think I would use you like that? What have I ever done to give you these kind of qualms about me?"

"Oh, I don't know. Made me fall in love with you and then tossed me out like I was garbage?"

He froze as her words registered, and so did she. "That's not what happened."

"I know." The look on her face said otherwise, though.

"You never loved me."

"You don't get to tell me how I felt."

"You never loved me," he insisted again, a little shocked at how shaky his voice was. How shaky he felt inside. "You betrayed me."

"I didn't betray you. I was caught between two untenable positions—"

"Being with me was an untenable position?"

"Don't put words in my mouth!"

"I'm not. Maybe you should think before you speak."

"God!" She made a sound of total exasperation as she headed out of the kitchen and back toward the front door. "I told you this wouldn't work. You need to leave."

He grabbed her arm, spun her around to face him. "I'm not going anywhere."

"Well, you're not staying here."

He raised a brow at her. "Wanna bet?"

"You need to go!"

"I'll go when you come with me."

"I'm not going anywhere with you. Not now, not ever again!" She was breathing fast, skin flushed and chest heaving. Tendrils of hair had escaped from the wild updo she'd pulled it into and burned like flames around her face.

They were in the middle of a fight and never had she looked so beautiful, so enticing, so delectable. A part of him wanted to shake her but a much bigger part wanted to take her. To shove her against the nearest wall and plunge himself inside her until she forgot every objection she had about him and he forgot every problem he had with her.

Until the past didn't matter anymore.

Until nothing mattered but the fire burning so brightly between them.

He reached for her before he could stop himself, pulled her body flush against his. She cried out, her hands going to his shoulders—to cling, to push him away? He couldn't tell. And by the way she arched against him, he didn't think she could, either.

Her breathing was harsh, her nipples peaked against his chest, and all he wanted to do was slip a hand between her thighs and find out if she was as turned on as he was. If she was as wet and hot for him as she'd been last night.

Overwhelmed with desire—with lust for her that just wouldn't go away—he lowered his head to take her mouth with his. And she almost let him…right up until she shoved at his shoulders hard and ripped her body away from his.

She stumbled back a few steps, staring at him with wide, bruised eyes.

He didn't follow, no matter how much he wanted to. Didn't grab hold of her and pull her back into his arms where a part of him was convinced she belonged. No, when it came to sex—to intimacy—between them, there was no way he would take that choice away from her. No matter how much he wanted her. No matter how certain he was that she wanted him, too.

"Get out," she told him, her voice low and broken.

"I can't. I need—" You, he almost said. *I need you.* Which would have been a disaster on so many levels. He could barely admit to himself how wrapped up in her he still was. There was no way he would admit it to her.

"Find somebody else to lie for you." She threw the words at him. "I won't do it."

Her words snapped him out of the sensual haze that had enveloped him the moment he'd touched her. He had a problem he needed a solution for.

Except, he'd already found a solution, hadn't he? His solution was her. Not just because she was one of the best in the world at what she did, but because—despite everything—he trusted her not to screw him over with this. It was a startling revelation after everything that had passed between them, but that didn't make it any less true. He knew she'd screwed him over once, knew that she'd stood by and watched first as he'd struggled to find out who was responsible for the diamond theft that had nearly ruined his business, and then again as he'd struggled to cover up for her father and keep him safe despite the industry's cries for his head.

But this felt different, and though he'd argued against it at first, now that he was here, staring into her eyes, he knew she wouldn't screw him over. Not on this and, hopefully, never again.

"You owe me," he told her, standing his ground even as she attempted to shove him toward the door.

She froze. "That's not fair."

"Do you think I give a damn about fair right now? My business is on the line. You owe me," he reiterated. "This is how I want to collect."

She turned pale, pressed her lips together so tightly that they turned nearly white. She shook her head, stepped back, but the look in her eyes told him he almost had her. "I can't just drop everything. I have plans—"

At the mention of her date, his patience abruptly ran out. He'd be damned if she turned her back on him because of some other man. Not after last night. And not when he was standing here, almost begging her for her help.

"Break your damn plans," he growled. "Or—"

"Or what?" she demanded, chin raised in obvious challenge.

He'd been about to suggest taking her straight to the

airport after her date, but her obvious belief that he was threatening her pushed him over the edge. If that was what she expected of him, then that was what he'd give her. "Or I'll break them for you. I'll break this new identity you've assumed wide-open, tell the school, the press, anyone who will listen who you really are. Then where would you be?"

"You wouldn't dare."

"You'd be surprised what I'd dare."

"If you did that, you wouldn't get your expert testimony."

"Yes, well, according to you, I'm not getting that testimony anyway. So, tell me, what have I got to lose?"

"You're a real bastard, you know that?" Her eyes were fiery hot as they glared up at him, but that only made the wet sheen of them stand out more. The knowledge that he'd brought this strong woman to tears made him feel like the bastard she'd called him, and for the first time since she'd pissed him off, he wondered if he'd had more to lose than he'd imagined.

"Look, Isa—"

"I'll do it," she interrupted, brushing past him. "But then, you already knew that, didn't you?"

He didn't know whether to be relieved by her acquiescence or upset by it. His father had taught him from an early age to go after what he wanted—no holds barred—but Marc had always tempered that ambition with care. Until now.

There was a part of him that wanted to tell her to forget the whole thing, to pretend he hadn't come here and threatened her. But then where would Bijoux be? This article would hit them hard. It wasn't just about what he wanted or needed. Bijoux employed thousands of people—where would they be if he let the *LA Times* deal such a crippling blow?

It was that thought that kept him quiet as Isa swept down the hall. "Where are you going?" he asked.

"To pack a bag. If that's all right with you?" He winced at the tone—and the look on her face. How she managed to look imperious dressed in sweats and a ragged tank top, he would never know.

He didn't answer her question—he knew a minefield when he heard one. Instead, he settled on a simple "Thank you."

"Oh, don't thank me yet. You may think you have the upper hand here, but if so much as one of your diamonds is the wrong composition, I'll crucify you in the press myself. And to hell with the consequences."

He watched her go and couldn't help smiling, despite her very deliberate threat. The fire was back—and he was glad. Despite their past, despite everything stretching between them, he never wanted to be the one to make Isa cry.

Ten

"Which mine are we going to first?" Isa asked as the pilot of Bijoux's private jet came over the intercom to announce that they would be landing in Kugluktuk in approximately twenty minutes. They were the first words she'd spoken to him since they'd gotten on the plane in San Diego, seven hours before.

"We'll go to Ekaori today and then tomorrow I'll take you to Vine Lake and Snow River."

She nodded, because that was pretty much what she'd been expecting. Ekaori sourced diamonds for numerous jewel companies, as did Vine Lake. But Snow River sourced exclusively to Bijoux. It was the newest diamond mine in the Northwest Territories—had only been operational since 2012—and was owned and operated by Bijoux Corporation itself. If anything suspicious was going on, that was where she would expect it to come from. So much easier to pull off a con—or a heist—when you were the one in control of the source material.

As they descended, they hit pretty impressive turbulence. She tried not to let it bother her—she'd flown into Kugluktuk to tour the mines numerous times in the past few years and it was always the same. They were only a hundred or so miles from the Arctic Circle, and the weather up there, even in the middle of summer, was always unpredictable.

Marc, she noticed, was making a valiant effort not to notice the turbulence, either. He kept working, one hand scrolling through the touch screen on his laptop while he glared at the screen. But his other hand was clenched around the armrest as if his will alone was the only thing keeping the plane in the air.

It didn't surprise her that the turbulence made him nervous. He was such a control freak that putting his fate in the hands of someone else had to grate, even at the best of times. Doing it now, as the plane dropped and bucked, had to be awful for him.

Before she could think twice about it—and about all the reasons she was still angry at him—she leaned forward as far as her seat belt would allow and placed her hand over his tense one. Then she squeezed gently.

He was sitting directly across from her, so when his eyes jerked up at the contact, they clashed immediately with her own. She didn't say anything and neither did he, but she felt him relaxing a little more with each swipe of her thumb across the back of his hand.

"We'll be down soon," he said, his voice a little deeper, huskier, than usual. As if she was the one who was nervous.

"I'm not worried." Which was a big, gigantic lie—she was totally worried. Not about the turbulence or landing safely, but about being here, with Marc. About how her hand was still resting on his and how good it felt to touch him. About the fact that, despite everything he'd done—

and everything she'd done—there was a part of her that still wanted him. That would always want him.

The thought stung, had her stomach clenching and nerves skittering up her back. Because the only thing stupider than letting Marc Durand into her bed last night would be letting him back in again tonight. He didn't trust her, didn't want her—hell, he wasn't above blackmailing her when the situation called for it. So why on earth did her body still respond to him? Why on earth did she want to comfort him when he had *never* done anything to comfort her?

Feeling like an idiot—or worse, a dupe—she started to pull back. But Marc's other hand covered hers, trapping her fingers. "Please," he said. "Don't."

Again their eyes met, and though she didn't see nervousness in his gaze any longer—he wasn't a man who tolerated weakness, in others or himself—she did see something that had her breath catching in her throat. That had her errant nerves turning from ice to a dark and sensual kind of heat.

That should have had her sitting back, getting as far away from him as she possibly could. When things had gone bad with them last time—when she'd begged him not to prosecute her ailing father even knowing the request meant he'd lose so much of what he'd worked for—it had nearly killed her. Not the icy walk in the winter rain after he'd kicked her out, though that had been no fun. No, what had nearly destroyed her had been the knowledge that she had hurt Marc irreparably.

Because of his parents, who had always cared more for money and status than they ever had for him and his brother, Marc trusted few people. But he'd trusted her, had believed in her, and in the end she had torn that trust to pieces by picking her jewel thief father over him.

It wasn't her proudest moment—was, in fact, one that still kept her up some nights. But what else could she have done? Her father was old, frail, dying. How could she have turned on him? How could she have let him spend the last year of his life in prison when he'd dedicated his life to giving her the world? To showing her wondrous places and things and teaching her that money wasn't important. Adventure was. People were. Yes, he'd turned her into a thief at an early age, but that wasn't all he'd been. And though she'd rejected that lifestyle when she'd met Marc, that didn't mean she could reject her father. He'd been a great father and she'd loved him very much.

And so she'd turned on Marc—or, at least, that's how he saw it. She'd begged him to understand, begged him to love her as she'd loved him, but that hadn't been possible. Not when all he'd seen was her betrayal.

Outside the plane window, the ground grew closer, lush with greenery as far as the eye could see. The first time she'd flown to Kugluktuk had also been summer, and she'd been astonished at the lack of snow and ice, had figured that this far north the ice would never melt.

But that wasn't the case. Though the mountains in the distance were still covered with white—and pretty much always were—the land down here was verdant and alive. And would be until the end of August, beginning of September, when temperatures dropped significantly.

Not that it was exactly warm here, even in mid-July, she admitted after the plane had landed and they took the stairs down to the tarmac. The temperature was about fifty—or so her phone said—but the fiercely blowing wind made it feel a lot colder.

She shuddered and pulled her jacket more tightly around herself as she thought longingly of the woolen scarf she'd left on her bed. Since it had been in the high sixties the last time she'd been here in July, she'd figured she wouldn't need it. Big mistake—and one she probably wouldn't have made if she hadn't been so annoyed at Marc while she was packing. After all, it didn't take a brain surgeon to remember that weather near the Arctic Circle was bound to be unpredictable.

Something warm brushed against her neck and she jolted, glancing behind her.

"Here, take mine," Marc said as he wrapped a black cashmere scarf around her neck.

"It's okay. I'm—"

"Freezing. You're freezing. And since I'm the reason you're here to begin with, the least I can do is try to keep you warm. Now, come on." He took her overnight bag from her and, with a hand in the center of her back, guided her toward the waiting helicopter.

She should pull away—she knew she should. After all, she was still furious with him for forcing her to come up here when she was still reeling from the way he'd made love to her and then walked out on her. He'd all but admitted that he'd had sex with her in an effort to get her out of his system. And then he'd blackmailed her into coming here to look at his diamond mines.

She should be telling him to go to hell, should be running as far and fast as she could in the opposite direction. What she shouldn't be doing is taking his scarf—and melting into his touch.

With that thought firmly in her mind, she pulled away. Started walking faster. And did her best to ignore the way she could still feel the imprint of his hand burning against her back.

The helicopter ride to the first mine was short—and a lot less windy than any she had ever been on before. Of course, that was because Marc had access to the best of everything—including a top-of–the-line helicopter that felt about as luxurious as a limousine.

They came into Ekaori from the north. She saw the huge, circular pit mine from quite a ways out. Her first glimpse of the mines from the air always startled her and today was no different. It looked much more like a whirl-pool carved into granite than it did a functioning mine. But the huge opening in the land was because of the sur-face mining that had been done for years, before the di-amonds had been exhausted and they'd been forced to expand underground.

They landed on the helipad right next to the main build-ing and Marc climbed out first, before extending a hand to help her. She didn't need his help, but she took his hand anyway. Out of politeness, she told herself as she moved past him. Not because she wanted to feel the brush of his warm skin against her own.

The general manager of the mine was obviously ex-pecting them—he was waiting right next to the helipad, with a huge smile on his face as he greeted Marc. She'd been to this mine no less than five times and had never seen Kevin Hartford up close, let alone had him meet her helicopter. But then, she'd never traveled with the head of the largest responsibly sourced diamond corporation in the world, either.

Marc had obviously told Kevin what she would need, because after a few minutes of polite chitchat in the outer office, he took her directly into the lab, where techni-cians laser cut a serial number and the lab's symbol—a small polar bear cub—directly onto each and every jew-elry grade stone. It was the first step in a long series that enabled regulators, and consumers, to track a diamond from the mine through production all the way to the store where it was sold.

Kevin also handed her a large binder with printouts of every serial number given to every diamond that had gone from the Ekaori mine to Bijoux in the past three years.

There were a lot of numbers.

He then led them to the screening plant, where they watched as thousands of pounds of rock were screened by machines and then by people for kimberlite deposits, the substance that created most diamonds. After the kimberlite was separated out, a second, more involved screening took place to find the actual diamonds.

She took samples from the rock and the kimberlite so that she could map the mineral content when she got back to GIA. Part of her wondered if the sampling was superfluous—after all, she had mapped the mineral content of this mine, and all the mines up here, numerous times, as had any number of other diamond experts. But Marc's business was depending on her doing this completely by the book, and so she would do just that. After nearly costing him his business once, she would be as careful as possible during this trip.

Though she would never admit it to him, especially after he'd blackmailed her into helping him, she did owe him for what he'd done for her father—and for the hit Marc had taken. The least she could do was make sure that her investigation of his diamond sourcing was beyond reproach.

By the time they were done with their tour of the lab and business facilities, it was too late to go down into the mine. Which was fine with her—she'd been in this diamond mine before and there was nothing new she needed to see. Besides, all the important documentation and identification work began once the stones were pulled from the rubble and tagged as either industrial or jewelry grade.

Marc hadn't said much during their time at the lab, taking a backseat as she asked questions. But once they were back in the helicopter, he turned to her and said, "I know you didn't want to do this, but I really appreciate you coming up here with me. I knew you were the right choice from the very beginning, but after watching you today, I'm so appreciative that you agreed to help me."

He looked and sounded completely sincere, and though there was a part of her that couldn't help wondering about his motives, she couldn't help responding to the warmth in his voice—and his eyes.

"I'm just doing my job, Marc."

"I know. With the way I coerced you into coming, a lot of people would consider you justified in using the opportunity to retaliate. You could destroy me if you wanted to and it would be no less than I deserved for how I've treated you."

"I would never do that!" She was shocked that he'd even think it. "I don't lie, especially not about something like this—"

"I know," he said again. This time, he was the one who covered her hand with his own. "What I'm trying to say, and obviously doing a crappy job of it, is thank you. I'm grateful for your help."

She stared at him for several seconds, completely nonplussed. This Marc, humble and open and kind, was the Marc she'd fallen in love with all those years ago. The Marc who'd held her and laughed with her and made plans for a future with her. And though she'd promised herself just that morning that she would never let her guard down around him again, Isa could feel herself wavering. Could feel her resolve crumbling as quickly as her defenses.

Which was why, when the helicopter landed in the back parking lot of one of the two hotels in Kugluktuk, she quickly gathered her things and stepped outside. While Marc spoke with the pilot about picking them up in the morning, she made her way into the hotel and registered for their rooms.

By the time he made it in, she had the keys to both rooms in one hand and her overnight bag in the other. She held one key out to him. "I guess I'll see you in the morning," she told him with a forced brightness she was far from feeling.

He raised a brow and for a second, she forgot how to breathe. Why did he keep doing that? she asked herself furiously. He was always gorgeous, usually able to curl her toes with only a look or a touch. But from the very beginning, whenever he had raised that damn brow of his, looking half questioning and half amused, it had made her heart beat too fast and her breath catch in her throat. The fact that it was still doing that, even after all this time and everything that had happened between them, made her take a step back in a futile effort to put enough distance between them.

"I thought I'd buy you dinner," he said. "The hotel has a pretty good restaurant, and the Coppermine Café across the street has great fried chicken."

"Actually, I'm kind of tired. I didn't get much sleep last—" She broke off in the middle of the familiar excuse as a wicked grin split his face. Of course he knew she hadn't gotten much sleep the night before—he'd been the one who'd kept waking her up to make love, over and over again, until now, hours later and thousands of miles away from her small beach cottage, she still couldn't get the scent of him off her skin.

"We can make it quick," he suggested. "We'll put our bags in the room and then—"

"No!" The word came out more forcefully—and more panicked—than she'd intended. But she wasn't stupid. She knew her weaknesses, knew that if Marc kept smiling at her, kept touching her, she'd end up in bed with him despite her resolution to keep her distance. And no matter how good he was in bed, no matter how much she enjoyed making love to him, she just couldn't go there again. Not if she wanted to come out of this situation with some semblance of her heart, and her life, intact.

Six years ago, she'd loved Marc desperately. She'd been caught between him and her father—between a rock and the hardest place possible—and she'd made the only choice she could make. But that didn't mean she hadn't loved Marc, didn't mean she hadn't grieved for him even after he'd ripped her out of his life without a backward glance.

She understood what last night was for him—a chance to exorcise her once and for all—and she needed to remember that. More, she needed to let the way he'd touched her and kissed her—the way he'd loved her—last night be enough.

It *was* enough, she told herself as she took another stumbling step backward. It had to be. She would pay her debt and then she would walk away, conscience clear and heart whole.

Or at least, that was the plan. A plan that would be totally derailed if she had dinner with him, followed by a glass of wine in his room and another night of the most amazing lovemaking a woman could imagine. Oh, he'd only asked her for dinner, but she knew him. She knew the look in his eyes, knew the way his mind worked, and she had no doubt that if she didn't run now, she'd find herself flat on her back under him before the night was out.

"I think I'll just get a snack from room service and then turn in," she told him. "I'm beat."

He didn't look happy now, his eyes clouded with obvious displeasure. But short of wrestling her into the restaurant, there was nothing he could do.

Except, it seemed, drive her absolutely crazy in the few minutes he had left with her tonight.

"All right," he said. "I guess I'll have to settle for taking you to breakfast in the morning." He reached past her to press the up button on the elevator, and though there was plenty of room, he made sure that his hand brushed against her side as he did so.

She bit back a gasp, telling herself the sudden shock of heat radiating from his touch was only because he was hot and not because he heated her up. She didn't believe it, but then, she didn't have to. She just had to pretend.

Fake it till you make it.

That was the motto she'd learned growing up. She might not be much of a liar, but she was a hell of an actress. Growing up the daughter—and accomplice—of the most renowned jewel thief in the world, she'd had to be.

Fake it till you make it.

And that was the same motto she'd lived by when Marc had kicked her out six years ago. For weeks, months, she'd been so morose that most days it had taken every ounce of energy she had just to climb out of bed. But her father was dying and she'd needed to be there for him even if she couldn't be there for herself. Which was why she'd pasted on a smile and pretended that everything was okay even as she was shattering into so many pieces she didn't think she'd ever put them back together again.

But she *had* put the pieces back together, she reminded herself as she stepped onto the elevator. And gorgeous smile or not, sexy eyebrow raise or not, she wasn't going to give Marc Durand the chance to change that. He'd broken her once—or, more accurately, they'd broken each other.

This time around, she'd forego the pleasure. And in doing so also forego the pain. In her mind, it was more than an equal trade-off.

Eleven

He didn't know what was going on with Isa, but whatever it was, he didn't like it. Marc glanced around the Snow River Diamond Mine, owned and operated exclusively by and for Bijoux, and did his best not to scowl with displeasure. Not at the mine, or at the questions Isa was asking, but at the way she had spent the entire day barely acknowledging that he existed. After yesterday, he'd hoped things would be different between them.

Oh, he was the first to admit that yesterday had not gotten off to a good start—how could it have when he'd rolled out of bed with Isa only to tell her that he'd slept with her to banish the ghosts of their shared past? And then he'd blackmailed her into helping him. Definitely not a good move in anyone's book. She'd been furious and had every right to her anger.

But on the plane, she'd seemed to soften. She'd remembered the fact that he was a nervous flyer and had tried to comfort him through the turbulence. She'd even smiled at him, let him touch her as they'd gotten off the plane. As the day had worn on, he'd seen her move from being an angry ex-lover to a consummate professional determined to do her job—even if doing that job meant helping the man causing her anger.

Her kindness had made him feel terrible, had made him determined to apologize for the way he'd treated her—and to make it up to her. She'd let him apologize, had even seemed to take it in the spirit he'd intended it. But then, when he'd wanted to take her to dinner as a kind of peace offering—and to continue the conversation they'd started earlier in the day—she'd frozen him out. Had, in fact, gone so far as to all but slam the door of her hotel room in his face. And since he'd made it a policy never to lie to himself, he had to admit that the rejection had stung.

Which was absurd. He was okay with her rejection piquing his pride, okay with it annoying him. But to actually be hurt by it? That he didn't understand. Because he didn't love Isa anymore, hadn't loved her in a long time. He'd made certain of that.

Sure, he wanted her, but what red-blooded man wouldn't? She was gorgeous, smart, kind, with a killer body and a wicked sense of humor. But just because he desired her, just because he respected the professional life she'd built for herself, didn't mean he was falling for her again. And it sure as hell didn't mean that he *loved* her.

She was doing him a huge favor and being absolutely incredible about it, but that didn't mean he would ever be stupid enough to fully trust her again. And he sure as hell wouldn't be stupid enough to fall for her, no matter how much his body craved hers.

He watched as she charmed his general manager, a grizzly old man by the name of Pete Jenkins. Until now, Marc had pretty much considered Pete completely uncharmable, but somehow Isa had managed it within an hour of meeting him. A couple smiles, a few well-placed questions and she had the diamond industry veteran eating out of her hand.

Marc would be lying if he said the knowledge didn't make him wary—especially since it hadn't taken much more effort on her part to have Marc wrapped around her finger all those years ago. But his wariness wasn't enough to make him keep his distance, especially when she once again gave him a wide berth as she said her goodbyes and made her way back to the helicopter that would take them to the airport, where his plane waited.

He almost hurried to catch up with her, almost grabbed her hand and spun her around so they could have it out right there, and to hell with who was around to witness it. He probably would have done just that—had actually started up the path to the helipad after her—when Pete called his name.

Tamping down the annoyance that was quickly turning to fury, Marc turned back to his GM with the closest thing to a smile he could muster. "What's up, Pete?"

"I was wondering if you'd had time to look at the expansion plans yet? We've got about eighteen months before the surface dries up, but we've got to get started building the underground tunnels if we don't want the mine to come to a screeching halt in the not so distant future."

"I have looked at the plans," Marc told him. "And there are a few things I'm not happy with, so I sent the architects back to take a second try. They're supposed to have them ready for me in a couple weeks—I figured we'd talk about it then."

Pete scratched his chin, nodding thoughtfully. "It's the block caving measurements, right?"

Marc nodded, not the least bit surprised that Pete had

picked up on the same problem he had. "The spacing is way off for this mine. It would work over at Ekaori or some of the other mines, but the veins of kimberlite are very different in this part of the Northwest Territory."

"The pattern they wanted to dig for those tunnels was going to end up costing a lot more than it needed to."

"It was. My geologist and I were also concerned about the maze of them based on the mineral composite of the land. Things are different up here than they are at Ekaori. The last thing I want is a cave-in—you know worker safety is the most important thing to me."

"I do. It's why I wanted to speak with you. I figured we'd be on the same page, but it never hurts to check."

"No," Marc agreed. "It never hurts to check."

He bid goodbye to Pete and headed back to the helicopter, even as he ran the GM's parting words around in his head. No, it never hurt to make sure both parties were on the same page. Especially when one of those parties was a stubborn redhead with a sharp mind and a curvy-as-hell body.

Isa continued to give him the cold shoulder on the helicopter ride to the airport, and though it grated, he took it. It was a short ride and not very private, considering they were in the same cabin as the pilot. He would wait until they were on the plane, where he'd have plenty of privacy and plenty of time to ferret out why she'd started avoiding him when he thought they'd been making progress.

He figured he'd start subtly, ask her questions that would force her to talk to him. After all, if it was business related, she couldn't very well refuse to share her thoughts. This was a business trip, after all.

Except…best laid plans and all that. By the time they were onboard his plane, luggage stowed and seat belts fastened for takeoff, he was seething. And when she took the seat farthest away from him and refused to so much as glance his way, his temper exploded.

"What the hell is wrong with you?" he demanded, unfastening his seat belt and stalking toward her just as the plane hurtled into the air.

"What are you doing? You need to sit down!"

"What I need is for you to stop treating me like I'm a cross between Jack the Ripper and Attila the Hun."

At that moment the plane hit some turbulence and it was sheer will alone that kept him standing, legs locked and arms crossed over his chest as he stared her down. They hit another bump a few seconds later, and he ignored that one, too—refusing to give in to the turbulence, or his uneasiness with flying, now that he had Isa cornered.

"I'm serious, Marc. You're going to get hurt—"

"I'm serious, too, Isa. And I find it rich that you're concerned with me getting hurt when you've spent the last day doing your best to pretend I don't exist."

"That's not true—"

"It's absolutely true and I want to know why. If you're mad at me, I get that. You have every right to be. But don't freeze me out. Yell at me. Call me a bastard again if that's what you want to do. But don't ignore me."

"I'm not mad at you."

"Oh, yeah?" He lifted a brow. "Because it sure feels like that from where I'm sitting."

"You're not sitting. That's the whole point."

They hit more turbulence on their way up and the plane bounced a little, shimmied. At the same time, the pilot came over the intercom reminding them to stay seated with their seat belts fastened until they reached cruising altitude.

"Do you hear that?" Isa demanded. "You need to sit down!"

He moved closer, bending over so that he rested a hand

on the armrests on either side of her and his face was in hers. "You need to talk to me."

"Damn it, Marc." She reached out a hand, splayed it over his chest, as if she planned to push him into a seat if she had to. But the moment she touched him, heat shot through him. Covering her hand with his own, he tried to ignore the fact that he'd gotten hard from just the warmth of her hand on his chest.

It might have been harder to ignore if Isa's breath hadn't hitched in her own chest—and if her pupils hadn't been completely blown out. Add to that the fact that her skin was flushed. Her hand trembled where it rested against his heart, and it didn't take a genius to figure out that she was as turned on by the contact as he was.

"Isa." Her name was ripped from him as he threaded his fingers through hers. "Talk to me."

She turned her head away, looked out the window at the blue sky where they were breaking through the clouds. It was late, nearly ten o'clock at night, but here, near the Arctic Circle, it was as bright as if it was the middle of the day.

She contemplated the sky for long seconds and though he wanted to push for an answer, wanted to push her in general, he waited for her to find the words she needed. It had always been like this when they fought—him shoving at her verbally and her responding by pulling into herself until she had the perfect argument figured out in her mind.

This time, it didn't seem to work, though, because when she spoke it was in little more than a whisper. "I don't want to do this."

"Don't want to do what? Talk to me?" He should probably move back, but he moved closer instead, until his face was only inches from her. "I thought we were getting somewhere yesterday, thought we could be—"

"What? Friends? After everything that's happened between us, you thought you'd just apologize and then we could be friends?"

The virulence in her voice had him rearing back. Maybe he'd read her wrong—maybe the signs he'd taken for arousal had really been nothing more than anger. That didn't make sense, though. Not when she gasped at his touch. And not when she responded so beautifully when they were in bed together.

"Friends might be a stretch," he admitted after several long seconds passed in silence. "But I thought, maybe—"

The pilot chose that moment to interrupt, announcing that they had reached their cruising altitude and that they were now free to move to the more comfortable sofas at the back of the plane.

Isa sprang out of her chair like a jack-in-the-box, nearly knocking into him in her haste to get away.

Except he wasn't letting her go that easily, not when he was so close to getting answers. And not, he admitted, when he was so hard that walking was going to be a problem.

"Where do you think you're going?" he demanded, grabbing her wrist and spinning her around.

"Away from you," she muttered.

"It's a little late for that, isn't it?" He started walking, bumping her breasts with his chest, her abdomen with his erection, her thighs with his.

She backed up a step for each one he advanced, through the narrow row of seats and across the aisle, until her back was pressed against the plane wall and her front was pressed tightly against his own.

"Why are you doing this?" she asked, her voice broken, breathless.

He might have felt bad, might have retreated, if his leg

wasn't between her thighs and if her hips weren't moving restlessly against the thigh he had pressed against her sex.

"Because I've never stopped wanting you." The answer slipped out of his lust-clouded brain. "Because I don't think I ever will."

"It's not enough," she said, even as she arched her back and pressed her breasts more firmly against his chest.

He could feel her nipples, peaked and diamond hard, through the thin fabric of her blouse and his T-shirt. He groaned, rubbed his chest against her breasts once, twice, then again and again as her breathing turned from shallow to ragged in the space between one heartbeat and the next.

"It's more than enough," he told her, bending his head so his mouth was right against hers. Each one of her trembling exhales left her mouth and entered his. "It always has been. Always will be."

"Marc." This time when she said his name it was more plea than protest.

"I've got you, Isa. I've got you, baby," he muttered right before he took her mouth in a kiss it felt like he'd been waiting years for instead of mere hours.

Twelve

She shouldn't be doing this, shouldn't be letting Marc do this. But as his lips took hers, his tongue stroking, slowly, languidly, luxuriously against her own, Isa didn't care about shouldn't. She didn't care about the past and she didn't care about the future, didn't care about how much this would hurt when the plane landed and she was once again alone. All she cared about—all that mattered—was the way Marc felt. The way he made her feel, as if her whole body was electrified. As if she could do anything, everything.

Her arms crept up of their own volition, wrapping around his neck and pulling him closer, closer, closer, until every inch of her was pressed up against some part of him. Mouth to mouth, chest to chest, sex to sex.

It felt so good.

He felt so good.

"Isa, baby," he murmured against her lips. "I want—"

"Yes." She ripped her mouth from his, pressed hot kisses against his jaw, his throat, the sensitive spot behind his ear. "Whatever you want, yes."

It must have been the affirmation he was waiting for, because with one last kiss, he pulled away from her. She made a low, confused sound in the back of her throat, but he just grinned wickedly as he wrapped his hands around her hips, cupped her bottom in his palms and lifted her against him.

"Marc." It was a moan, a plea, a desperate cry for more even as she wrapped her legs around his waist, pressing her sex firmly against his own.

He took her mouth again, his lips hot and firm and desperate. Then he was shifting her weight a little, turning, walking through a door toward the back of the plane. When she'd first come aboard, she'd wondered what was back here. Now she knew—it was a small bedroom, complete with a large bed with a black comforter and gray silk sheets.

He never faltered as he walked her backward across the room, never so much as shifted what she considered her pretty substantial weight. Instead, he kept kissing her, skimming his mouth over every part of her he could reach—every inch of exposed skin—and she marveled at his strength, at the feel of all those hard muscles against her own softness.

And then they were at the bed and he was dropping her into the center of it with no warning and a wicked, wicked grin. She gasped at the short fall—and at the sudden lack of contact with this man she should know better than to fall for again.

She did know better, she told herself as she reached for him, her fingers tangling in the soft cotton of his T-shirt.

She just didn't care, not now when Marc was here, hot and hard and as desperate for her as she was for him.

She pulled him down on top of her, then rolled the both of them until she was the one on top, her thighs straddling his hips as she looked down at him. "It's my turn," she told him a little breathlessly.

He just smiled, lifting that damn eyebrow of his that was responsible for so much of the trouble she'd found herself in. "You look like you expect me to protest."

"Aren't you?"

He smirked then, a small twist of his lips that sent heat streaking through her. "I have you on top of me, warm and willing and—" his fingers skimmed between her legs, rubbed at her sex "—wet. What in the hell is there for me to protest about?"

He looked as though he wanted to say more, but she leaned forward, stopped him with a kiss that had her hands trembling and her brain melting within seconds. Then she was pulling, tugging, yanking at his shirt, desperate to get it off so that she could touch the warmth of his skin, the hard press of his muscles.

He laughed darkly, even as he half sat up in an effort to help her divest him of the garment. And then she was touching him everywhere—his shoulders, his heavily muscled pecs, his too-perfect abs—licking her way across and down his beautiful, glorious body.

He gasped when she got to his belt, arched against her, shuddering, as her fingers—and her tongue—dipped below the waistband of his jeans.

"Isa, baby—"

"I've got you," she said, mimicking his words from earlier as she unbuckled his belt, unbuttoned his jeans. She slid to the floor beside the bed, tugging at his shoes, his pants, his boxer briefs, until Marc was spread out before her, gloriously, perfectly naked.

He muttered a curse, reached for her, but she shook her head, pushed his hands away. "It's my turn," she said again, right before she took him in her mouth.

He groaned, low and long and tortured, his hands tangling in her hair as she pulled off in order to press long, lingering kisses along his length. He shifted, arched his hips, tangled his fingers in her hair. She knew what he wanted, what his body was all but begging for, but she wasn't ready to give it to him, not yet. Not when he'd spent so much of their last night together tormenting her.

But then he cupped her jaw in his big, calloused hand, tilting his head so he could look down at her with his dark, dazed eyes and she lost the last of her willpower. Leaning forward, she took him deep.

Her name was a hoarse cry on his lips as he arched and moved and shuddered against her. It had been a long time since she'd done this to a man—over six years, to be exact—but she still remembered what Marc liked and how he liked it. Still remembered the taste of him as he spilled on her tongue.

She wanted that again.

He was close, so close, and she stroked her fingers across his taut stomach as she prepared to take him over the edge. But Marc was having no part of it. Grabbing her hand in one of his, he held it tight as he used his other hand to coax her mouth back up to his.

"I want to feel you," she protested against his lips. It was a halfhearted protest, though, because he was stroking her breast, pinching her nipple between his thumb and middle finger even as his index finger stroked back and forth against the hardened tip.

She gasped, arching against him. It was all the encouragement he needed. Dropping to his knees beside her, he kissed her slowly, thoroughly, passionately. For long seconds she couldn't move, couldn't think, could barely breathe. She was completely enthralled, completely under his spell and she wanted this moment to go on forever.

Then he was lifting her, spreading her out on the bed before him like a feast. "Marc," she gasped, her fingers clutching at his shoulders as she tried desperately to pull him over her.

Pleasuring him had driven her own need to the breaking point and she wanted—needed—to feel him inside her. But Marc had other ideas. Leaning forward, he pressed hot, wet, openmouthed kisses against her sex.

She lost it then, her fingers twisting in his hair as she arched against his mouth. His wicked, wonderful mouth. He slipped his hands beneath her, cupped her bottom and lifted her hips so there was no escape, no surcease, no moment to catch her breath. There was only him, only Marc, and the crazy pleasure he gave her.

Again and again, he brought her right to the edge of madness, of desire. Again and again, he refused to let her go over. By the time he pulled away to slip on a condom, she was an incoherent mess. Begging, pleading, promising him anything and everything if only he would—

He slid inside her then, his mouth pressed to hers even as he moved a hand between them and stroked her. That was all it took. She went off like a rocket, her body exploding with pleasure that went on and on and on.

Marc rode her through it, his hand and mouth and body taking her higher and higher until she was lost. Lost in pleasure, lost in him, lost in what could be between them if they let it. She gasped out his name, pulled him closer, closer, closer. When he thrust against her one final time, when he took her mouth in a kiss so deep, so passionate, so all-consuming that she could do nothing but surrender to it—to him—she went over the edge again. This time she took him with her, and nothing had ever felt so good.

Thirteen

"Just an FYI, Marc," the pilot's voice came over the loud-speaker in the plane's small bedroom. "We'll be landing in half an hour."

Beside him, Isa stirred, but didn't wake. Pushing up on an elbow, he stared at her, mesmerized, for long seconds that turned into longer minutes. She was beautiful like this.

Actually, she was always beautiful, with her pale skin, dark eyes, luscious hair and even more luscious body. But there was something about her when she was sleeping that made her even more appealing. Maybe it was the fact that this was the only time he'd seen her truly relaxed since he'd walked into her classroom the other day. The only time she'd allowed him to see the real Isa behind Isabella, the woman with the tight braid, quiet demeanor and impressive credentials.

Or maybe it was the vulnerable curve of her full lower lip that made her so enticing. Or the soft pink flush to her normally ivory cheeks. Or the way her hand curled around his biceps, as if, even in sleep, she was trying to hold him. God knew, he hadn't slept for that very same reason. He'd been afraid of falling asleep while holding her only to wake up and find out that the tenderness and the passion had been a dream. Or that somehow, when he loosed his grip, she would slip through his fingers like kimberlite silt.

He didn't want that to happen this time. He didn't know what he *did* want to happen—didn't know, really, how he felt for her outside the need that continued to claw at him. No matter how many times he had her, he continued to want her. Wanted her still, right now. He wasn't ready to let her go.

Maybe that made him a fool. Hell, it probably did considering everything she'd put him through—and everything he'd put her through in return. But as he lay there, watching her, touching her, the past didn't seem to matter nearly as much as it once had. Nothing mattered but Isa and the way she made him feel.

"Fifteen minutes until landing, Marc. You guys need to take your seats if you haven't already."

He leaned over, pressed the button on the nightstand that allowed him to talk to the cockpit. "We'll be out in five, Justin."

Then he woke Isa, forcing himself to gently shake her shoulder until her chocolate-brown eyes looked up at him in confusion. "I'm sorry, baby. We've got to get dressed. We're about to land and we need to take our seats."

She blinked, rubbed her eyes. Then shoved her thick mass of red hair away from her face as she sat up slowly. He froze, watching as the sheet slipped down her torso to pool around her hips.

She looked like a goddess.

Like a vision.

Like the sexiest wet dream he'd ever had.

Eyes sleepy, lips swollen, cheeks warm and flushed. Yes, she looked like every fantasy he'd ever had—*would* ever have. Her hair was long and wild out of its braid, tumbling down around her shoulders and over her soft, full breasts. But he could still see the strawberry pink of her nipples, the pale curves of her breasts. He wanted to taste, wanted to bend his head and pull her nipple between his lips just to hear her make those broken, breathless sounds one more time.

He was actually leaning forward, mouth parted and eyes focused on the prize, when she slapped a hand on the center of his chest. "How long until we land?"

Her voice was low, husky. He grinned and grew hard yet again. The sound of her voice reminded him of what it had felt like to be in her mouth, in her throat. Of what it had felt like to slide between her wet, swollen lips as she took him deep.

"Oh, no," she continued, scrambling out the other side of the bed. "Judging by the time, I'm pretty sure we can't go another round."

She was right, they didn't have time. But that didn't seem to matter to his insistent hard-on. If he was being honest, it didn't matter much to the rest of him, either. Not when he ached to once again feel her skin, her softness— her sweetness—against every part of himself.

But there was something incredibly sexy about watching a well-satisfied woman shimmy into her clothes, her movements slow and languid as she stepped into her jeans or pulled her sweater over her head. He loved how pale her skin was, loved that her breasts and stomach and thighs bore small love bites and patches of whisker burn. Loved that she looked like she'd spent the past several hours being made love to by him. Loved even more that she looked like she belonged to him.

The thought pulled him up short, had him reaching for his own jeans and yanking them on a little harder than necessary. Because wanting Isa, enjoying making love to her, was one thing. Hell, he'd probably still want her when he was dead. But thinking about her belonging to him again—that was dangerous. Really dangerous, considering how much he liked the sound, the look, the feel of it.

"Here." Isa's voice pulled him back from his minor freak-out, and he realized she was holding his shirt out to him. She was also looking at him a little strangely, but he refused to let himself dwell on it. Not when his head was already filled with so many conflicting thoughts.

They finished dressing in silence, but when Isa opened the door and started back to their seats, he grabbed onto her waist, pulling her back to him. He didn't know what to say—he couldn't tell her that he loved her, but he didn't want to leave her with a "wow, that was fun," either. And so he let his actions speak for him, nuzzling his way up her neck and along her jaw.

She relaxed then, a tension he hadn't even recognized leeching slowly out as she melted against him. The moment was broken when Justin's voice came over the intercom, reminding them to take their seats.

They did just that, and this time when Isa reached for his hand it wasn't because of turbulence. And for now, for this moment, that was enough.

An hour later, Isa waved as Marc pulled out of her driveway. She watched him go, hands shaky and with a lump in her throat as big as the entire Ekaori diamond mine.

What had she done? she asked herself as she closed her front door. What was she *doing*? More, what was she *thinking*?—if you could even call the choices she'd made the past few hours "thinking." Which she wasn't sure she could. Committing emotional suicide, probably. Being stupid, absolutely. But thinking? No, she hadn't been thinking—was desperately afraid, in fact, that she'd left her brain somewhere over Northern Canada.

What else could it be? She'd left her house a little more than twenty-four hours ago, determined that Marc would never touch her again. Yet here she was, back home in the early hours of the morning, what was left of her mind preoccupied with Marc and her body pleasantly sore and well used.

So well used. She closed her eyes as images of Marc bombarded her. On top of her, beneath her, on his knees at her feet. His hands on her hips, on her breasts. His mouth skimming over her stomach, over her sex. Kissing her, taking her, loving her… No!

She slammed a mental door on those thoughts. Whatever crazy chemistry was between her and Marc, whatever disaster she was courting by being with him, she wouldn't go that far. She wouldn't call it love, not on his side and definitely not on hers. She didn't know yet what she would call it, but she would not call it that.

Love was too painful—she'd learned that six years ago. She'd loved him then and all it had gotten her was heartbreak. This time she would be smarter. This time she wouldn't let herself care, not like that. Not like her whole heart, her whole soul, depended on him.

Deep inside, a little voice whispered that it was too late. That she was already in way over her head. But she shut it down, refusing to listen. Not right now when she could still feel Marc moving over her, inside her. Not right now when she was too exhausted, too vulnerable, to know what the truth was, let alone face it.

Deciding to let it go for now so that she could maintain some semblance of sanity, Isa carried her overnight bag into her bedroom. She dropped it next to her dresser and then flopped face-first onto the bed.

She could barely breathe with her face buried in the mountain of pillows, but she didn't have the energy to so much as turn her head. It was five thirty in the morning and she had an early lecture at eight—the first of two back-to-back classes that she normally loved since it meant getting done early on Mondays and Wednesdays. At the moment, though, it seemed like torture to expect her to be showered, dressed and out of the house by seven. Not when she had barely slept in the past three days.

She could lay that at Marc's door, too, she told herself. Along with the soreness that came with using muscles long neglected and the love bites that kept popping up in new places, he was also responsible for Saturday's sleepless night, staring at the cracked and stained hotel ceiling. And God knew, Friday and Sunday nights were definitely his fault. The forty-five minute nap she'd gotten after he'd made love to her for hours didn't count as a good night's sleep.

Her phone buzzed in her back pocket and, against her better judgment and the protests of her screaming muscles, she reached for it. Glanced at the text that had just come in. It was from him. Of course it was—who else would be texting her at five thirty on a Monday morning? On this very particular Monday morning.

Marc: Just wanted to say thank you again for making the trip to Canada.

That was it? Thank you for coming to Canada? She waited a few seconds, staring at the screen expectantly, hoping for another text to come in. Because surely that couldn't be it, right? Surely, he hadn't spent the better part of a six-hour plane trip taking her apart, orgasm by orgasm, only to send such a ridiculous text as follow-up?

Seriously, why even bother?

She waited another minute, her stomach clenching despite the fact that she told herself that it didn't matter. Over and over again. Until she almost believed it.

After all, what was he supposed to say? If she'd tried to text him, she wouldn't have a clue what to say—or how to refer to what had happened between them.

Not when there were no established parameters.

Not when the closest thing they had to a relationship had ended six years before.

She'd just put the phone down on the bed next to her—and reburied her face in the pillows—when the damn thing buzzed three more times in quick succession.

Marc: I'll see you at Bijoux headquarters at noon today.

Marc: That is, if we're still on?

Marc: Also, I had a really nice time. Hope you did, too.

A nice time? He'd had *a nice time*? What the hell was that supposed to mean? A trip to the park was a nice time. Going to a movie with a friend was *a nice time*. Totally fabulous, completely toe-curling, absolutely mind-blowing sex was *not* a nice time. It wasn't close to being a nice time. And while she'd already established that she didn't know what it *was*, she definitely knew what it wasn't. And it simply was not a nice time.

Shouldn't Marc know better than to call it that? Especially if he wanted more fabulous, toe-curling, mind-blowing sex in the near future. Which, judging by the way he'd kissed her goodbye, he absolutely did. Although why he'd want sex with her when it was merely "nice," Isa didn't know.

She debated answering him, debated sending him a text that was as innocuous and insipid and soul-crushing as the ones he'd just sent her. She could tell him what a "nice time" she'd had, as well. Might even mention how much she'd enjoyed the seven orgasms—not that she'd been counting—that he'd given her. She could even say that she looked forward to running into him sometime at GIA. That would certainly get her point across.

But in the end, she did none of those things, because the truth was, she didn't have it in her to play games with him. She never had—she just wasn't the kind of person who enjoyed dangling a guy on a line simply to watch him squirm. It was why she and Marc had done so well together in the time they'd been a couple. He'd never been interested in artifice, either, had always been a straight shooter. Or at least until now. Until he'd sent her a text that said he hoped she'd had a nice time.

As if.

Though she'd originally flopped into bed with the hopes of catching an hour of sleep before going to work, she was now way too wound up to even think about sleeping. Her brain whirred at a hundred miles a minute as she tried to figure out just how big a mistake she'd made in sleeping with Marc, not just for one night, but two.

So instead of taking a nap, or sending him a return text, or relaxing after what had been a mentally and physically grueling thirty-six hours, she forced herself to get up and go into the bathroom for a quick shower.

After drying her hair and putting on a quick swipe of mascara and lipstick, which was all the fuss and muss she had the energy for today, Isa settled herself at her kitchen table with her laptop and a cup of coffee. Once there, she pulled up all the known data she had on the diamonds coming out of Canada—including the composition of impurities from the different mines. And then she got to work.

Besides serial number and mine symbol, the impurities were the best way for a gemologist to determine where a diamond actually came from. For example, African diamonds had impurities that were made of certain kinds of sulfides while Russian diamonds had impurities made largely of nitrogen. Unfortunately, or fortunately depending on how you looked at it, Canadian diamonds had neither—and very few impurities in general when compared to other diamonds in the world. This was good for the Canadian mine owners, because while the diamonds coming out of Canada only accounted for about three percent of the bulk sales of diamonds worldwide, they also accounted for over eleven percent of the revenue. This was due to their exceptionally high quality and low level of inclusions.

Which was very nice for Bijoux and all of the other companies with mines in Canada, but it certainly was a pain for gemologists trying to prove definitively that a diamond came from any of those mines. Which wasn't to say that it couldn't be done. It could. Just not in the normal way used to identify most diamonds.

The first thing she had to do was check the serial numbers on a wide range of the diamonds in Bijoux's vault, making sure that they matched up exactly to the ones from the Canadian mines. She had the binder, but she also had a USB stick with each of the serial numbers on it—she inserted it into her computer and downloaded the information into a program on her hard drive that would allow her to easily match up the numbers from the mine with the numbers on the diamonds in the Bijoux vault.

Next, she pulled up all the documentation on which levels were mined at which times, including the exact dates each level was declared extinct. As she did this, she checked to make sure that she had the exact mineral makeup of the soil found at each level. In most cases the soil compositions were similar or identical, but every once in a while one of the lower levels differed significantly from what was above it. Tomorrow, when she was in the lab, she would compare the silt samples she'd taken with her previous documentation—and then she'd look at the makeup of the Bijoux diamonds and ensure the probability that they came from these mines.

It was an important step in the process—both were— but the fact of the matter was neither would give her, or Marc, the definitive answer they were looking for. Diamond sourcing was a tricky business, made so by the nearly identical mineral composites of the stones no matter where in the world they were found, and by the less than up-front business dealings so many of the world's diamond traders engaged in.

Which left her with one final thing she was looking for—one final thing to try. It couldn't be forged, couldn't be erased and was, quite often, overlooked by people trying to pass off blood diamonds as conflict free: hydrogen atoms or isotopes on the surface of the diamond. These atoms were deposited on the stone by rainwater that sank into the ground around the stones before they were mined. They clung to the surface of the diamonds. Once there, they were notoriously hard to remove.

While the presence of isotopes wasn't enough to prove that a stone came from a certain region, the chemical makeup of the individual isotopes definitely could. The exact makeup of rainwater differed from place to place around the globe and because of this, the hydrogen isotopes deposited on the diamonds also differed so that each region had very different isotopes attached to its diamonds.

Years of research—from her and other gemologists who specialized in diamonds—had provided a pretty decent mapping of these isotopes. On her computer, she stored a breakdown of rainwater composition in all the major diamond mining areas—including Canada's Northwest Territories. So while she would, of course, scrutinize Bijoux's records, serial numbers and the impurities of their diamonds, it was these isotopes that she was counting on to prove Marc's case. Or disprove it.

She really hoped it wasn't the latter.

Not because she was sleeping with him and not because she had a past with him, but because—despite how things had ended between her and Marc—she had always thought of Bijoux as one of the good guys. In an industry that was both highly dangerous and highly monopolized by companies that didn't mind trading in blood, terrorism and child labor, Bijoux had always been clean. Or, it had been for at least as long as Marc and Nic had been in control. From the very beginning, the brothers had run the company differently from most other gem companies, ensuring that they did as little harm, and as much good, as they possibly could.

Both men had a strong environmental conscience and an even stronger social conscience, both of which leant themselves to making sure the Bijoux mines were the safest in the world, both ecologically and for their workers. For years, she'd held up Bijoux in her classes as examples to strive for in a business that far too often lacked heroes. After all, gems were pretty but for most companies, the mining—and trading—of them was anything but.

To find out that the Durand brothers had given up on the beliefs they'd always espoused—simply to line their already too-full pockets—would destroy the last of her already flagging idealism.

With that thought uppermost in her mind, Isa spent the next hour and a half poring over every piece of recorded data she had, or could find, about the diamond mines that Bijoux did business with.

She looked at hydrogen isotopes until her eyes crossed.

Memorized the mineral makeup of silt at all the mine levels Bijoux had bought stones from in the past eighteen months.

And she prayed, entirely too hard for a woman who shouldn't care one way or another, that when she started combing through Bijoux's vaults, everything would match up.

Because if it didn't... If it didn't, she would end up breaking a lot more than just Marc's company. She was going to break his heart. And no matter what lies she fed herself to get through the day, if that happened she was very, very afraid that she would break her own heart, as well.

Fourteen

"Has Isa found anything yet?" Nic asked the second he hit Marc's office on Monday afternoon.

"She's only been here three hours," he told his brother without looking up from his computer screen, where he was going through what felt like a never-ending string of emails that had accumulated in the day and a half he'd been in Canada. "Give the woman a chance to do her job."

"I'm giving her a chance. But we're getting down to the wire here. We only have a few days before the *LA Times* runs that article and I want to debunk them well before their Thursday night deadline hits."

"Believe me, you can't possibly want that any more than I do. But that doesn't mean we need to stick our noses in the vaults every five minutes and pressure Isa. She's already working overtime—we only got back from Canada this morning and she has to be exhausted." God knew, he was. "But she's here and she's doing her best to find the truth."

"Wow." Nic stopped pacing long enough to glance at his brother with raised eyebrows. "Since when did you start defending Isa Moreno?"

Since…since… He didn't know when. "What does that matter? We should be worrying about finding whatever traitor planted a false story with the *LA Times*."

"Believe me, I am worrying about that. But despite my seemingly carefree disposition, I'm actually quite good at worrying about more than one thing at a time." Nic grinned. "So hit me, big brother. What's going on with you and Isa?"

"Nothing's going on between us!" Marc barked, suddenly uncomfortable with the turn the conversation had taken. He'd barely wrapped his head around the fact that he was back to sleeping with Isa. He sure as hell didn't need anyone else—especially his smart-ass little brother—poking at their relationship right now.

"You sure about that? Because you seem awfully touchy for a man who's got nothing going on. Then again, maybe that's *why* you're touchy—"

"I am not touchy! And if I were, it would be because I'm waiting, just like you, to hear something from the vault. I know three hours is nothing when it comes to the job Isa has to do, but that doesn't mean I like the wait. And it sure as hell doesn't mean I like the silence."

"Amen to that, brother," Nic said, plopping himself down in one of the chairs opposite Marc's desk. Before Marc could blink, his brother had kicked his feet up onto the polished wood of his desk and leaned his very expensive antique chair back on its hind two legs.

"Could we say amen to you not killing yourself? And you not breaking my chair into fifty ridiculously small pieces?"

Nic just rolled his eyes. "You worry too much."

"I'm CEO. It's my job to worry too much." Marc glanced at the clock for what had to be the tenth time in as many minutes. He was trying to keep his calm for his brother, but the truth was, he was a wreck inside. He knew that none of his stones were conflict diamonds. He knew that they all came from the Canadian diamond mines that were ecologically sound and paid high wages. But that didn't keep him from wondering, or from worrying. Not when there was some traitor in their midst, slipping ridiculous stories to the *LA Times*. If they could make up a story about Bijoux dealing in conflict diamonds, what would stop them from bringing in a few of the blood-soaked diamonds to cement their case?

Just the thought made him sick. And had him pacing the same route back and forth across his office that his brother had just vacated.

"It's going to be fine," Nic said, sounding as if he was trying to convince himself as much as he was trying to convince Marc. "Besides, no news is good news. Right?"

"Right." Marc forced himself to think through the worry. "Lisa is with Isa in the vault and I'm sure she'll let us know the second Isa finds something that proves—or disproves—the article."

"She isn't going to find anything that proves the article," Nic told him confidently. "Because there's nothing to find. So what are we worried about?"

"Absolutely nothing," Marc told him, even as he contemplated pacing another lap around his office.

Except Lisa chose that moment to stick her head in. "Any news?" she asked as both brothers came to attention.

"Why are you asking us?" Marc said in disbelief. "You're the one who's been hanging out in the vault with our expert for the last three hours."

"Actually, I left her a couple hours ago. I had a meeting

to go to and she was pretty much lost in her own world anyway."

"A meeting? You left Isa alone in the diamond vault because you had a meeting to go to?"

"I left Dr. Moreno alone in the diamond vault." She looked uncertain for the first time. "Is that a problem? It's standard protocol with experts from the GIA—if anyone can be trusted, it's them. Besides, what's she going to do? There are fifty cameras in that vault, plus high-resolution imaging machines that record every single thing on your person as you enter and exit. Even if she wanted to steal something—which I'm sure she doesn't—she couldn't."

Marc knew Lisa was right, knew he'd set up the best security for his vault that an unlimited budget and years of expertise in the business could provide. Not to mention the fact that Isa had never stolen from him. Her father had, but she hadn't. Not six years ago when they were together and not anytime since.

Still, he exchanged an uneasy look with Nic. His brother had been her greatest champion, in the past and the present, and yet even he looked uneasy at the idea of Isa being alone in the vault. Marc moved swiftly for his office door.

"What's wrong?" Lisa asked. "Where are you going?"

"Don't worry about him," Nic said as Marc walked out the door, obviously covering—for him or for Isa, he didn't know. Nor did he care. "He's just uptight about this whole thing."

"We all are. I know you think it's just your reputations on the line, but it's all of ours. I stand behind every single diamond in that vault and the idea that some jerk has the nerve to lie about it—lie about us—makes me crazy. Especially when he's too much of a coward to accuse us to our faces. He has to go behind our backs, to some sleazy journalist, and try to discredit us that way."

Marc missed Nic's response to her diatribe as he was already halfway to the elevator. He told himself that everything was fine, told himself that he was paying Isa an exorbitant amount of money to certify his diamonds—money that she would be a fool to risk for the one or two diamonds she might actually be able to sneak out of the vault unseen.

And still he couldn't help cursing the elevator for taking as long as it did to arrive. He believed in Isa's integrity, believed she would never steal from him. Hell, he even believed that she hadn't stolen anything from anyone since she'd first met him; she had access to gems at GIA all the time. And still the little voice in his head urged him to hurry. Still he wanted to be up there in that vault with her. Not because he really thought she'd steal from him, but because he wanted to avoid having her face the temptation.

Most jewel thieves were like junkies—they couldn't stop even after they'd amassed enough money to retire. Isa's father had been like that. The man was a millionaire many times over, and dying of cancer to boot, but still he hadn't been able to resist the big score. Still, he'd stolen from his daughter's fiancé without remorse or concern. Hell, for a long time, Isa had been like that, too. When she'd begged him to keep her father out of jail, she'd told him about the thrill she'd always felt when stealing. Had told him how much she loved the adrenaline rush but how she'd given it up because the rush she got from being with him was so much bigger, so much more than she could ever get from stealing.

Now, after all these years, he knew she'd meant that. Knew she wasn't like that anymore. But what if the temptation was too much? What if she wanted to take one little stone, just to see if she could do it? Just because she wanted to?

Sometime in the past few days—probably right around the time she'd agreed to help him despite his over-the-top behavior—he'd forgiven her for what had happened all those years ago. Had forgiven her for choosing her father over him and leaving him, and his company, to flounder in the wake of it all. The man was her father, after all, and he'd needed her more than Marc had. But just because he understood, didn't mean he fully trusted her. Forgiven her, yes. But trust…he was still working on that.

If she did this, though, if she stole from him after everything they'd gone through, he knew he would never be able to forgive her. Hell, he wasn't sure he'd even be able to look at her again.

Maybe he should be grateful for this opportunity, he thought, as the elevator doors finally opened. It would show him what she was made of before he risked anything else on her. But the fact of the matter was, he wasn't grateful. He was scared. Not because he was worried about losing inventory, he realized as he swiped the badge that would take him to the top floor of the building where the vault was housed. But because he was worried about losing Isa. He'd already lost her once. He didn't want to go through that again, no matter what lies he'd told himself about his feelings for her when they were in Canada.

The elevator dinged to announce its arrival at his destination, and Marc waited impatiently as the doors slid open. They seemed to be taking three times longer than usual to do so, and though he knew that wasn't actually the case, it didn't make the wait any easier.

Finally, the doors opened and he all but launched himself out of the elevator and down the hall toward the main vault, where Isa was supposed to be working. In his haste, he nearly ran over Victor, one of their most accomplished diamond techs and a man who had worked his way up from stone polisher to management in a very short amount of time.

Victor smiled, called hello, but Marc was in too big of a hurry to do much more than nod at the man. And then he was around the corner, staring at the blinking lights that meant the vault was occupied but that its security—sans motion detectors—was fully engaged. He didn't know whether to be grateful or concerned.

In the end, he was neither. He kept his mind blank, open, as he swiped his badge and his fingerprints. Then he entered his personal code for the vault and waited for the thick steel door to unlock. It only took a couple of seconds, but it felt like an eternity.

Then he flung the door open and rushed inside like a crazy person. And all but bumped into the makeshift desk Isa had set up near the opening of the vault, a desk that held a laptop, a microscope and a small drawer of diamonds. She had one of the diamonds under the microscope, had obviously been studying it intensely when he'd barged in. Now she was studying him intensely.

"You okay?" she asked, putting the diamond down and pushing back from the table.

"Yeah, of course. I'm fine," he said because, really, what else could he say? *I freaked out because I thought you were going to steal from me*? Or how about, *I'm still freaking out because you've been alone in this vault for two hours and I don't know if you've pocketed anything*? Yeah, right, because either of those would go over so well. "I just wanted to check on your progress, to see if you'd found anything one way or another."

She laughed, even as she reached a casual hand out and rubbed his shoulder. "I know it's nerve-wracking, especially with that article hanging over your head, but nothing of any value can be done in an afternoon, especially in a vault of this size, with this many diamonds. If you're lucky, I'll be able to discuss my findings on Wednesday, but more likely it's going to be Thursday. And that's only if I spend every working hour here while my substitute teaches at the GIA."

She didn't sound bothered by that fact, but he was suddenly—overwhelmingly—swamped by guilt. Guilt for thinking, even for a second, that she was a thief. And guilt that she was working so hard to reassure him when he'd been suspecting terrible things about her. It didn't seem fair. Not when he'd been the one to almost beg her to take this assignment. Of course, that was before he'd known she'd be left alone in the vault.

Searching for something to say to diffuse the awkwardness he felt he glanced at the diamonds spread out on the table in front of her. Then stiffened because, well, honestly, they were small diamonds. Easy to lose, easy to fence. Easy to pretend away if things weren't going her way.

"Is there anything you need?" he asked as casually as he could. "Anything I can get for you?"

"Not right now. Tomorrow I'll need access to your labs, but for now I'm okay here if you have other stuff you want to do. You know, like run a company." She smiled as she teased him.

"Actually, I thought I'd hang out here for a while, if that's okay with you. Just in case something comes up. You're doing Bijoux a huge favor and I'd hate for you to have to wait for something you need."

"I'm actually good. I'm doing the serial number check right now and will probably be on that for the rest of the day so I really won't have anything to report unless I find a stone with a mismatched number." She put a hand on his shoulder, squeezing gently in what he assumed she thought of as support. "It's *nice* of you to offer, but there's nothing for you to do right now."

He didn't like the way she stressed the word *nice*, as if he was missing something. Considering that was exactly what he was afraid of, it ratcheted up his suspicion, had him walking toward the end of the vault and retrieving a chair from the small display there. He carried it back to her, set it down a few feet from her desk. Then slid into it with an easy smile he was far from feeling.

"Even so," he said, pulling out his phone and pretending to be busy. "I've cleared the rest of my afternoon, so I'm at your service."

She shot him an odd look. "You're seriously going to stay here the whole afternoon?"

"The whole afternoon," he agreed. And though he felt guilty for his suspicions, he still wasn't moving. Not when she was trying so hard to get rid of him. And not when she was currently concentrating on some of the smallest diamonds in the vault. He didn't like the looks of it and while he wasn't stupid enough to tell her that, he also wasn't stupid enough to leave her alone in here like a kid in an unsupervised candy store.

Isa gave him a strange look as she settled back down at her desk and returned to work, but he pretended not to notice. Which was so much better than letting her see how nervous she made him…and on how many different levels.

Fifteen

Marc was acting weird. Not crazy, need-a-straitjacket weird or anything like that, but he was definitely a little off. She glanced at him out of the corner of her eye as she finally finished checking the last diamond in the current batch and placed it back in the blue velvet–lined drawer.

He wasn't looking at her, wasn't paying attention to her at all. Which was fine—he was CEO of Bijoux, after all, and she was sure he had a lot of work to do, especially considering the allegations leveled at the company—but it still made her feel funny. As if she wasn't important enough for him to pay attention to. Or, as he hadn't made any move to touch her since he came into the vault, as if what had passed between them over the weekend had never happened.

He hadn't even risen to the bait when she'd used the word *nice*...which made her feel even more as though he wanted to forget making love to her.

Having sex, she reminded herself a little bitterly as she carried the drawer back to its place and slid it into the long, slender opening in a wall that was covered with row after row, column after column, of just such drawers.

The Bijoux vault was organized by size, color and clarity—pretty much like any vault she'd ever been in. Sticking with the smaller stones of lesser quality she moved to her right two columns and pulled out a drawer that was second from the top, then carried it back to her makeshift desk.

Marc had yet to say anything, or even look up from his smartphone, where he was currently scrolling away like the weight of the world depended on how fast he moved his index finger. It annoyed her all over again—she didn't need much attention, but *something* would be nice. A smile. A few careless sentences. An acknowledgment that they'd spent the entire weekend together, working and making love.

She ended up slamming down the drawer on the desk a lot harder than she'd intended to.

The sharp crack echoed through the room and for the first time since he'd settled in the chair next to her, Marc looked up with a frown. "Everything okay?" he asked.

"Yes. Everything's *nice*." She stressed the word a second time, even knowing she was being something of a brat. But he was getting under her skin and though she knew it was her fault for letting him, she couldn't help it. If all he'd wanted was a two-night stand, he could have said so, right? He'd had no problem saying it after the first time he'd crawled out of bed with her on Saturday morning. Why hadn't he said something to the same effect this morning when he'd dropped her off? Something like, "I had a nice time, but with the work you're doing for Bijoux, I really think we should keep it professional from here on out."

She probably would have snarled at him, would definitely have thought he was a douche. But then, she'd decided sometime in the past hour that he was a douche anyway, so it's not as if he'd gained anything by playing his games. Whatever those games might be and whatever purpose he thought they might serve.

She didn't say anything as she got back to work, opening the drawer and pulling out a selection of diamonds in the quarter carat, slightly included range. As with the drawer she had just examined, these were some of the cheapest diamonds in the vault. While the drawer of them was worth hundreds of thousands of dollars, individually each was only worth a hundred or so.

"Can I ask a question?" Marc asked, and she looked up to find him studying her intently.

"Of course. That'd be nice," she answered.

His eyes narrowed to slits and she knew she'd pushed the nice thing as far as she would get away with. Which was fine, because the longer he went without calling her on it, the more like a spoiled brat she felt.

"Why are you dealing with only the small diamonds? Shouldn't you be looking at the bigger ones? If someone at Bijoux is playing fast and loose with serial numbers and countries of origin, they'd be more likely to make a significant amount of money by passing off a large diamond as conflict free rather than a small one."

"You'd think so, but my colleagues' and my experience has borne out the exact opposite to be true. Big diamonds are flashy, they draw more attention and so it's harder to keep a fraud going for any length of time. There's just too much scrutiny on stones over a carat, especially when they're VVS1 or VVS2. Everyone wants a look at stones that are only very, very slightly included.

"Whereas, with these stones, nobody pays much attention. They aren't very glamorous and they aren't worth very much money in the grand scheme of things, so people—jewelers, conflict-free experts, consumers—have a tendency to not pay as much attention to them. After all, who would go through the trouble of forging papers on a stone that's barely worth a hundred bucks? Especially if they only stand to gain a couple extra dollars on it?"

"Someone who's faking it on thousands of stones," he offered.

"Yes. Or, more likely, hundreds of thousands. Then the money suddenly becomes a lot more worth it."

"Yeah, I guess. If you don't mind selling your soul for a little profit."

He looked so disgusted that she couldn't help laughing. "I think you've forgotten the basics of Human Greed 101," she told him. "Not to mention the very foundations on which the diamond market functions."

"I wish." He flashed her his first real smile of the afternoon. "So that's why you're concentrating on the small diamonds. Because it's easier for someone to flip in a few fakes there than in the stones of significant size."

"Absolutely." She looked at him curiously. "Why else would I be spending all my time with these stones when the right side of the vault is filled with so many more beautiful ones? Which, incidentally, I will be getting to. But not until after I deal with these."

He shrugged, grinned at her. "No rush. I want both of us to be completely satisfied as to the validity of my stones' origins."

She nodded hesitantly, feeling a little like Alice tumbling down the rabbit hole as he shot her another blinding smile. Because this time when she settled back down to work, Marc didn't ignore her. Instead, he lifted his head often and smiled at her. Offered to refill the water bottle that rested, forgotten, on the corner of her desk. It was as if he was a different man than the one she'd spent the past hour with and she couldn't help wondering at the schizophrenic behavior. Especially when she'd convinced herself that his previous behavior had been because he wanted to make sure she got the hint about his intentions—or lack of intentions—about their relationship.

She still wasn't sure what was going on. After all, who wanted to waste their time on "nice" when they could be aiming for spectacular?

She didn't say anything to him, though, and he didn't bring it up with her—at least not until it was well after dark and the rest of the company had closed around them.

She was working to finish a drawer of half-carat stones and was hoping to get one more drawer done after that before calling it quits. But as she put the last VVS1 stone back into its drawer, Marc's hand covered hers. For the first time she realized he'd put his phone away and his chair back and was pretty much just hovering over her.

"I'll put this bunch back," he told her. "Why don't you get your stuff together?"

She glanced at her watch, surprised to find it was after nine. "Actually, I was hoping to do one more drawer before heading home. It shouldn't take me long—"

"Maybe not, but you look dead on your feet," he said. "Whatever you still have to do will be here tomorrow."

She thought about protesting—she had a limited amount of time and a lot of ground to cover—but she wasn't the only one who looked exhausted. He was hiding it well, but Marc looked like he, too, was feeling the effects of three nights without sleep.

"Yes, all right," she agreed. It only took her a couple of minutes to put her laptop away and gather the rest of her stuff. Then they walked out together, Marc making sure the vault was sealed behind them, the alarms and motion sensors all activated.

They were out of the building and almost to her car in the parking lot before he spoke again. "What kind of take-out do you like?"

"Takeout?" she parroted, the words so far from where her brain was that it took her a minute to process them.

"Food?" he said, his voice deep and amused. "I figured we'd grab something to eat on the way back to your place."

"My place?" she echoed.

He looked at her strangely, the warmth in his smile fading as he took in her total surprise at the suggestion. "Unless you'd rather not have a meal together?" he said, and she knew he was thinking about Saturday night, when she'd refused every overture he'd made to get her to eat with him.

"No, no. Takeout would be nice." This time, the word slipped out without her permission or attention.

But he picked up on it—of course he did—his eyes narrowing as he asked, "What is it with you and your preoccupation with the word *nice* today?"

She flushed a bright red, ducking her head as she tried to either avoid the question or figure out a way to answer him that didn't make her sound like a complete crazy person. But he wasn't having any of it, his fingers going to her chin and tilting her face up until her eyes met his.

She didn't say anything and neither did he and, of course, she cracked first. She always had when it came to him—how had she not remembered that until this moment? The way Marc noticed every small detail about her? The way he'd wait her out whenever he asked her uncomfortable questions, never getting bored or anxious, but rather pausing patiently for her to wrap her mind—and her courage—around whatever it was she wanted to say.

"I just—" She broke off, shook her head. "Any chance we can just leave that alone for now?"

He quirked a brow in that way that made her insane— with affection, with envy, with *lust*. "Pretty much no chance at all."

"Yeah, that's what I figured." She sighed heavily, shifting her weight. She shoved her free hand in her pocket. Anything and everything to kill time as she tried to figure out what she wanted to say. But in the end, though Marc hadn't grown impatient, she certainly had and she just blurted out the truth. "You said last night was 'nice.'"

He looked baffled. "When did I do that?"

"In your text message to me this morning. You said you'd had 'a nice time.'"

"And there's something wrong with that?"

Her embarrassment faded as annoyance took its place. "I don't know, Marc. Why don't we test it out? You take me home, make love to me, and then—on your way out the door—I'll tell you how nice it was."

He didn't say anything for long seconds, just stared at her as if she'd lost her mind. And maybe she had. At this point, she really couldn't tell. All she knew was that she didn't want him to drop his hand from her face, didn't want him to stop touching her. Ever. And that was a huge problem considering the fact that she'd been promising herself all along that she wouldn't fall for him again. That she wouldn't let herself love him.

"Seriously, sweetheart?" he said after a minute. He dropped his hand and she made some kind of noise at the loss of contact—half protest, half plea. He responded by wrapping her in his arms, pressing her body against his from shoulders to shins. "I was half-asleep and barely coherent and that's what you've been holding against me all day? Do you think maybe you could cut a guy some slack?"

When he said it like that, he made his words seem completely reasonable. But, still, before she got in any deeper, she needed to know. "You weren't trying to blow me off? To distance yourself from me?"

He lowered his head, pressed kisses to her forehead, her cheeks, her mouth. "Does this feel like I'm trying to distance myself?"

"No." She shook her head. It felt kind of wonderful, actually. Familiar, but not. Safe, but not—in the best possible way.

"Okay, then. Since that's settled, why don't you tell me what kind of takeout you want and I'll swing by and get it on my way to your place. If I'm invited, that is?" He was grinning, his eyes bright with mischief as he teased her. But she could see the uncertainty there, too, lurking behind the easy facade. Almost as if he was as weirded out and nervous about this thing between them as she was. Almost as if he had as much to lose as she did.

Just the thought had her breath catching in her throat, had her searching his face for signs of the same overwhelming feelings she was having. She found them in the crinkle of his eyes, in the soft corners of his smile, in the hand that wasn't quite steady on her arm.

And somehow the knowledge that she wasn't alone made everything better. She'd loved Marc Durand once, with every beat of her heart, with every ounce of her being. Losing him had nearly killed her, which was why she'd sworn never to repeat the mistake. And yet, here she was, after several strong warnings to herself, in the middle of the fall all over again. It wasn't a comfortable place to be, not by a long shot. But when he looked at her like that—all soft and sweet and *involved*—it wasn't a bad place, either. It was actually a little wonderful.

"I choose Greek," she told him. "There's a little place

two blocks over from my house. It's a hole-in-the-wall but the food is amazing."

"Greek it is, then. Text me the name and I'll find it," he replied, dropping one last, lingering kiss on her lips before pulling open her car door for her. "Drive safely."

She laughed. "Same old Marc."

"Hey. You used to like the old Marc."

He was right. She had. Right up until he'd tossed her out on her butt without so much as her apartment key. Unbidden, the memory of that long-ago night crept in—along with an uneasiness she refused to feel.

Not now, when Marc was looking at her with such warmth.

Not now, when she could feel herself melting into a puddle of warm goo at the look in his eyes.

And so she settled for a half-truth, as she wrapped her arms around his neck and pressed her mouth against the dark stubble on his jaw. "I still do like him."

This time she was sure it was his breath that caught in his throat, his heart that was beating way too fast. "Go," he said, after taking her mouth in a swift, hard kiss that set her nerves jangling and her sex pulsing. "Before I decide to take you right here in the parking lot with my security guards looking on."

She wasn't sure what it said about her that right then, at that moment, that didn't sound like such a bad proposition.

Still, she climbed in her car, let him close the door after her. And, as she drove home, she refused to think about the future. For the first time in her adult life, she refused to think about the consequences of what she was doing. Instead, she decided that, just this once, she would look before she leaped.

And pray that she landed on her feet.

Sixteen

Two days later, she was still leaping. And still falling, with no hint of the ground in sight.

It was wonderful and awful, exhilarating and terrifying, all at the same time. Especially since Marc seemed to feel exactly the same way.

Last night he'd invited Nic to come to dinner with them and she'd spent the two-hour meal laughing until her sides hurt. Even with the threat of the newspaper article hanging over their heads, Nic was just that kind of guy. He always had been, but she'd forgotten that in the years since she'd seen him last. Just as she had blocked out so much of her time with Marc because it was too painful to remember.

She was remembering it now, remembering all the fun they'd had together. The million ways Marc had to make her smile. The million and one ways she'd had to make him relax, no matter how stressful his day had been.

And now, as she walked up to his office, she couldn't

keep the triumphant smile from her face. She'd completed the last of her tests, had spent the entire day looking at hydrogen isotopes until her eyes crossed and her brain felt as if it would bleed out of her ears.

She'd crashed what was normally a ten-day certification process into five days and she was exhausted, completely wiped out. But none of that mattered because she had good news for Marc. It was news he already knew, of course, but it would still be a relief to him and Nic to know that she concurred. And that none of their employees had snuck something shady in under the radar.

Marc's assistant, a really nice guy named Thomas, waved her toward Marc's door as soon as he spotted her. "Go right in. He's been waiting for you for the last two hours."

Of course he had. He was that kind of guy. She'd told him she thought she'd be finished around four and her phone had buzzed with a text at exactly 4:01, checking to see if she was finished for the day.

She'd put him off for two hours as she ran more isotope tests than she ever had before—many more than the industry considered necessary. But she wanted this certification to be beyond reproach, wanted Marc to have the peace of mind of knowing there was no truth to the *LA Times* article at all.

After the debacle of their past, she owed it to him. More, she wanted it for him. He deserved it.

He and Nic and Harrison, one of the attorneys working on their end of the situation, were all gathered around Marc's desk when she walked in. And though they were chatting amiably enough, the tension in the air was thick enough to scoop with an ice cream spoon.

All eyes turned to her and she smiled, holding out to Marc the folder of documents she'd put together—and signed—certifying Bijoux as carrying only conflict-free diamonds. She would send him electronic copies of the same papers, but for now, handing him a folder felt more official. More real. She supposed she was old-school like that.

It must have felt official to him, too, because the moment he opened the folder and saw the first page, her lover grinned like a crazy man.

"We got it?" he asked, his voice slightly hushed despite the excitement on his face.

"You absolutely got it," she said.

Nic jumped out of his chair, pumped a fist in the air. "I knew it, baby! I knew that reporter had a bad source." He gave Marc a second to look over the documentation she'd provided, then ripped the folder out of his hands and headed for the door.

"Where are you going?" Marc demanded.

"To make a copy of this file. And then I'm going down to the *LA Times* myself and force-feed every single page of this to that jackal of a reporter. I hope she chokes on it."

"I feel obliged to warn you of the illegality of such actions," Hollister said. But he was grinning, and Nic just rolled his eyes and flipped him off, so she figured it was a long-standing joke between them. Which didn't surprise her at all—Nic was totally the kind of guy to skirt the rules just enough to make a lawyer like Hollister absolutely insane.

She started to sit down in the chair vacated by Nic, but Marc grabbed her and pulled her into his arms. Then he picked her up and actually spun her around his office, laughing the entire time.

"Yes, well, I guess I'll leave you to your celebrating," Hollister said. "Send me a copy of the report when you get it back from Nic. I'll make sure to have it messengered over to the editor of the *LA Times* before I go home tonight."

"I thought Nic was already doing that?" she asked as Marc finally set her back on her feet. "He looked like a publicity director on a mission to me."

"Oh, he is," Hollister assured her. "But I just want to cover all the bases. Make sure no one has a chance to say the verification—and our comment on it—slipped through the cracks."

He left the office after that, leaving her and Marc alone to grin stupidly at each other.

"I want to celebrate," he said, grabbing her hand and bringing it to his mouth. "I want to take you out somewhere fancy and ply you with champagne and chocolate and moonlight." He pressed several kisses to her fingers, before turning her hand over and doing the same to her palm and wrist.

Shivers of excitement went through her at the whisper soft contact, and she leaned into Marc. Let him hear the hitch in her breathing and let him see the way her hands were suddenly a little unsteady.

His eyes darkened and then he was kissing her, his lips and tongue and mouth devouring her own as need—hot and dark and overwhelming—flowed between them.

"Hold that thought," he growled when he finally ripped his mouth from hers. Then, grabbing a small remote from his desk drawer, he darkened the privacy shades on the windows until no one could see in. Then he strode over to the door, starting to close and lock it. But before he'd done much more than swing it shut, Lisa appeared, pale and disheveled.

"I need to talk to you," she said. She looked absolutely panicked, her face drained of color and her hands shaking as she made her way into his office without an invitation.

"What's wrong?" Marc asked, leading her to a chair. "Are you okay?"

"I'm fine," she told him, placing the tablet she held on the desk. "But the vault isn't."

Isa felt her stomach plummet to the floor, felt her heart stick in her throat. "What does that mean?"

Lisa pulled up a spreadsheet on the computer, gestured to it wildly. "It means we're missing several of the large, two-carat and above VVS1 diamonds. It means," she said, choking on tears, "that Bijoux has been robbed."

"That's not possible," Marc said, keeping his voice—and himself—as calm as possible.

"That's what I said when I went in to pack up several of the jewels for shipment this morning. But they're missing. I've checked and double-checked the logs. I've searched every drawer within five rows in both directions, just in case they were put back in the wrong place for the first time *ever*. I've even pulled up the security tapes and nothing suspicious popped at all. No one has been in that vault in the last three days who doesn't belong there."

"Three days? Is that the last time you saw those diamonds?"

"I saw them Saturday. I had just secured them in the vault when you called me into your office. I haven't checked them since—have had no reason to until today. No one except Isa has."

He could barely think around the suspicion—around the rage—that was seeping into him from all directions. This couldn't be happening again. It simply couldn't. It wasn't possible. Isa wouldn't do this to him a second time, not when they were finally starting to get somewhere. Not when he was finally beginning to move past her betrayal of six years ago.

Yes, he'd been suspicious enough to stay in the vault with her. But they'd moved past that. No way would she do this. And no way would he be so stupid that he didn't see it. Not when he'd been so careful. Not when he'd worked so hard to make sure she wouldn't fall victim to temptation while she was here.

While she was in his vaults.

He told himself not to jump to conclusions, not to let his suspicions run away with him. But still he couldn't look at Isa as he called up security and ordered the video for the past five days to be emailed to him.

"What can I do to help?" Isa asked from where she was standing, frozen, next to his desk.

He didn't answer. Didn't trust his voice, or the words that would spew out of his mouth.

Picking up his phone, he called his head of security. Demanded that the man meet Marc at the vault in the next five minutes. Then he grabbed his cell phone and the tablet Lisa had brought with her and made a beeline for the door and the elevator.

As if the machine understood the rage coursing through him—and the fact that Marc was one breath away from jumping out of his goddamn skin—the elevator came right away. He got on, waited for Lisa to do the same. But when Isa went to join them, he told her, "Don't."

She froze, eyes wide and cheeks pale. It was the last visual he had before the elevator doors slid shut.

He pulled up the video, had it running on the tablet before he even hit the vault floor. He kept it running as he did the usual security routine to open the vault, his eyes never leaving the footage as it ran through Saturday afternoon.

He paused it when Bob, his head of security, showed up. "Seven of the nearly flawless one-point-five-carat diamonds are missing," he told Bob, as he thrust the tablet at him. "Find out what the hell happened."

Before entering the vault, he called up the IDs of everyone who had entered in the past ninety-six hours. Lisa was right—there was no one suspicious on the list. Nobody suspicious but the woman who had spent the past three nights in his bed.

He blocked out the thought, along with the fresh wave of rage that threatened to swamp him, to pull him under. He concentrated on the job at hand.

"I want three pairs of eyes on the footage from every camera in this vault," he barked at Bob. "I want to know what happened in this room every second of the last ninety-six hours and then I want to know what happened in every other room on this floor. In the bathroom down the hall. In the only two damn elevators that actually reach this floor. And I want to know these things in the next four hours.

"I also," he continued, gritting his teeth and doing his damnedest not to bellow like a wounded bear, "want to know where the bloody damn hell my diamonds are. I want to know how they got out of the vault, I want to know how they got out of the building and I want to know where the hell they are right now!"

"Yes, Marc." Bob looked as pale as Isa had right before the elevator doors closed on her. Good. It was his damn job to make sure this didn't happen and now that it had… he damn well better figure out how to fix it.

Except it wasn't fair to blame Bob, the little voice in the back of Marc's head whispered. Not when Marc had knowingly, wittingly, brought an ex-thief into his building. Into his vault. Not when he'd trusted her despite her track record—and despite his misgivings. No, this wasn't Bob's fault so much as it was his. He was the one who had trusted Isa. He was the one who—after that first day in the vault—had given her more and more freedom at Bijoux. He had given her the run of the place because he'd begun to trust her again.

Because he'd wanted to believe in her, no matter who her father was. No matter what she'd done in her past.

Jesus Christ. Six years and he hadn't learned a damn thing. He was still a sucker for red hair, a sweet smile and a pair of chocolate-brown eyes. Still a sucker for Isa.

No, not a sucker, he told himself viciously as more of his security team swarmed into the vault. He wasn't a sucker. He was a goddamn fool. An idiot. A moron who deserved every bit of this. He hadn't learned the first time, hadn't been smart enough to keep from repeating his mistakes, so fate had stepped in to teach him a lesson once and for all.

Well, he'd learned it this time. Christ, had he ever. No way would Isa ever pull one over on him again.

Jesus, he thought even as he barked orders to start inventorying the drawers. They would have to eat the loss of those diamonds. He wasn't going to some insurance investigator with this story. They'd laugh him out of the building. After they crucified him, that is.

Provided nothing else was missing but those seven stones, it wasn't a big deal. They were nice stones, but they weren't anything spectacular. They sure as hell weren't worth enough that they would disrupt anything important, not even his profit and loss margins.

Three hundred grand retail, maybe. A hundred grand sold to a fence on the streets. That was it. A hundred thousand dollars. Is that what his love was worth to Isa? A hundred grand? Silly girl. If she'd stuck with him she could have had a lot more than that. She could have had everything that was his. He'd been so close to loving her again, so close to giving her anything and everything she could ever want.

And instead of loving him back, instead of caring about him at all, she'd done this. Stabbed him in the back even while she continued to make love to him.

His stomach clenched at the thought and for a minute he thought he was going to embarrass himself all to hell by getting sick. But he swallowed down the nausea, forced his body to take it just as he forced himself to take the pain of Isa's betrayal. Better to deal with it now than to sublimate it and give it the power to bring him to his knees later.

He did everything he could in the vault, issued all the orders that needed to be given at this first stage of the investigation. He supposed he could thank Isa for that, too. Isa and her father. If it hadn't been for the robbery six years ago, Marc wouldn't be as well versed in what needed to be done.

It took him nearly three hours to make his way back down to his office. Three hours in which he watched time-lapse video of every single person who had been in the vault since Saturday afternoon. Three hours in which he had to tell his brother that they'd been robbed, again. Three hours in which he stewed and brooded and grew angrier and angrier as the truth became clear. No one had been in this vault in the past four days who hadn't been in it hundreds of times before. No one had been in this vault who hadn't worked for his company for at least five years. Nobody, that is, except the woman who insisted on making a fool of him over and over again.

He didn't know what he'd find in his office, didn't have a clue if Isa had fled the premises or if she would be stupid enough to be waiting for him. Nor was he sure what it said about him that he didn't know which option he would prefer.

The choice was taken out of his hands, however, when

he pushed the door to his office open and found Isa curled up on his sofa, eyes wide and feet tucked under her.

She jumped up as soon as she saw him, crossed the room at close to a dead run. "Did you find out what happened? Does Security know where the diamonds went? Or how they were smuggled out? Or—"

She broke off when he held up a hand. "I'm going to ask you once, Isa, and then I'm never going to ask you again. Did you take those diamonds?"

"No, Marc. No! Of course I didn't. I would never do that to you. I would never do that to us."

He stared at her for long seconds, searched her face for sincerity. Then nodded. "You need to leave."

"Leave? But—"

"You need to leave now. I'll have accounting cut you a check for the work you did for me and then you need to get whatever things you have here and you need to leave the premises. Forever."

"You don't mean that."

"Oh, I mean it, Isa. I mean it more than you could possible imagine."

"Seriously?" she demanded. "It's been six years and we're right back here again?"

"Don't act offended. After all, you're the one who put us here."

"No, Marc. You're the one at fault this time. Because I didn't steal those diamonds."

"Stop talking!" he ordered her as fury threatened to swallow him whole. "Stop lying to me. I can take anything but that. I can take knowing you stole from me, but I can't take you looking me in the eye and lying to me."

"I'm not—"

"Get out!" he yelled. "Before I have you escorted from

the premises. Get out now and I'll have your check mailed to you tonight. Just get out."

"Marc, please—"

He whirled on her then, the rage breaking wide-open inside him. "Get the hell out, Isa, or this time, I really will call the police."

He walked over to the bar in the corner, poured himself a tall Scotch, and drained it in one long swallow. Then he poured another one and did the same thing.

When he turned around again, prepared to face Isa one last time, he found that she'd finally given him what he'd asked for. She was gone and he was alone. Again.

Seventeen

She didn't know what to do, didn't know where to go. Didn't know how to deal with the fact that her heart had just split open and broken into a million pieces. Again.

After she'd fled Marc's office, his words ringing in her ears, she'd run through the halls, down the stairs and out onto the grounds that stretched along the ocean.

And now, here she was, staring out at that ocean and wondering how, how, *how*, she could be in this position again. How, after everything that had happened six years ago, that the *two* of them could be in this position? Again.

She told herself to just leave.

Told herself to walk to the parking lot, climb in her car and drive away.

Told herself that this time, she wouldn't look back. Ever.

Marc had turned on her again. The thought slammed into her over and over. With each step she took on the sand, with each wave that rolled in, the knowledge that he didn't trust her ripped at her.

He thought she was a thief, thought that after everything that had happened these past few days—after everything that had happened six years ago—she had actually turned around and stolen from him.

As if she would do that. As if it was even possible for her to hurt him that way.

Then again, maybe it wasn't so far-fetched that he believed it. After all, he had no problem hurting her. Had no problem turning his back on her six years ago and no problem turning his back on her now—despite all the sweet words he'd spent the past few days, and nights, whispering in her ear.

Just the memory of these few stolen days had her feeling like her whole body would break apart. Like her skin would crack under the weight of her sorrow and her limbs, her organs, her *heart* would fly right out of her in a million different directions.

Isa wrapped her arms around herself at the thought, tight around her middle, her hands clutching her sides. And she walked along the shore, right where the water met the sand. Right where the infinite waves swamped the crumbling shore.

She walked and walked and walked.

And as she did, she lambasted herself for all the things she'd done wrong. For all the hope she'd let herself feel even when it was idiotic and dangerous…and painful. So painful.

She'd known better, even as she was doing it. Had known better than to trust Marc after what had happened between them six years ago. More, she'd known that *he* would never be able to fully trust *her*.

Which was the real problem, wasn't it? The fact that

no matter what she did, no matter how she'd changed her life or how she'd tried to help him, he was never going to get past who she'd been. Never going to see her for who she really was.

It was a hard truth to swallow, one made harder by the fact that she had never stolen from him. Not then, and not now.

No, she hadn't stolen from him, she forced herself to acknowledge as she kept walking, her shoulders hunched against the wind blowing in off the water. But she'd certainly thought about it six years ago. It would be a lie to pretend otherwise.

That was who she'd been then, what she'd done. Not because she needed the money—her father had stolen enough through the years that her children's children would probably never need for money—but because she'd wanted the thrill.

The old Isa had been an adrenaline junkie, raised by her jewel thief father after her mother passed away. She had loved the game, the con, the robbery more than anything else in the world. Except her father…and eventually, Marc.

She'd met him at a big society party she'd been casing, had fallen for him hard the moment he'd handed her a glass of champagne with a smile and a quip. And that damn raised eyebrow of his. She still remembered what he'd said to her at that moment—would probably remember it until she died. Because even as it was happening, she'd known that it was one of those life defining moments.

She'd looked up into his shining sapphire eyes, ripe with amusement and desire, and she'd realized that she wanted to know more. Realized that she wanted to know *him*.

And so she'd ditched the friends she'd been with, ditched her plans to steal the big, fat Poinsettia Ruby that had drawn her to the party in the first place. She wasn't going to lie—it had hurt a little to walk away from the huge, thirty-five-carat stone surrounded by ten carats of flawless diamonds—but she'd done it. Despite the fact that it had been right there, just waiting for her to pluck.

Okay, so maybe it had hurt more than a little. Maybe it still did.

But that night she'd wanted Marc more than she'd wanted the stone. More than she'd wanted to please her father. More than she'd wanted the life she had. And during the six months they'd had together, she'd continued to want him more than anything.

She'd given it all up, cold turkey. She'd missed it—of course she had. For most of her life, stealing big, flashy jewels and pretty paintings had been as natural to her as breathing. But she'd wanted what she saw in Marc's eyes, what she felt in his arms, more than she wanted the dark, shiny, illicit thrill that came every time she'd pulled a heist.

Her father hadn't understood—he'd never wanted anything more than he'd wanted the rush of the next job. Had, for the longest time, thought she'd been casing Marc, trying to find his weakness. Trying to get inside Bijoux's vault, where—at the time—two of the most perfect diamonds ever found were being housed. The Midnight Sun, a colorless and flawless forty-carat Russian diamond valued in the tens of millions and Hope's Fire, a twenty-seven-carat nearly flawless diamond whose value came as much from its rich and violent history as it did its quality.

Marc had been preparing to auction off both of them—at the time, he'd spent the first few years of his career moving Bijoux away from blood diamonds and firmly into the conflict-free arena. A huge event was planned—a huge gala that she had contributed time and expertise to helping him pull off—with the proceeds going to a char-

ity that helped children in areas where blood diamonds
were mined.

Her father had been thrilled when he'd found out, had
been convinced that she was just using Marc to find an
in with the diamonds. When he found out that wasn't the
case, found out that she was with Marc because she loved
him and wanted to spend the rest of her nonthieving life
with him—he'd been furious. He'd accused her of turning her back on him.

And she hadn't been able to argue, had she? Because
she *had* turned her back, not on her father, but definitely
on the life he'd given her. The life he'd raised her to want,
to expect, to relish.

She should have known then what would happen, what
he would do. In many ways, her father was a child, as
thrilled by the chase, by the hunt, as he was by the shiny
baubles he stole. And once he was focused on a score, nothing short of the apocalypse could tear him away.

What she hadn't realized—what she'd been too naive at
the time to understand—was that in falling for Marc, she
might as well have painted a target on him and his business. In giving him her attention, her love, her *loyalty*,
she'd made him and his diamonds the focus of her father's
attention. In fact, when she'd told her father that she wasn't
going to steal anymore, that she was going straight and
building a life for herself as a normal person, she'd pretty
much put a giant red *X* over Marc.

When the diamonds turned up stolen and Marc's whole
business—his whole life—had gone to hell, she'd known
who had done it. Of course she'd known. She'd stolen with
her father since she was nine years old, had recognized the
earmarks of a Salvatore job as easily as she recognized her
own face in the mirror.

That was where she'd made her second mistake. Because she hadn't told Marc then what she knew. Hadn't gone to him and explained who she was and who her father was and offered to help him get the stones back. Instead she'd gone to her father, and tried to convince him to return the stones. He'd refused—of course, he'd refused. It was, in its own way, a matter of honor to him. Marc Durand had stolen something precious from him and he had returned the favor.

Even after that encounter, she still hadn't told Marc the truth. How could she when doing so would not only send her dying father to prison but would also make Marc look at her with scorn, hate, disgust. She hadn't been able to do it then. Hadn't been able to ruin all of her dreams, all of her happily-ever-after fantasies, in one fell swoop. Even though in keeping her own dreams alive, she'd destroyed Marc's.

And perhaps she would have gone on living a lie forever if things hadn't gotten so bad for Marc. She liked to think the guilt would have made her confess eventually, but after everything that had happened these past few years, she was honest enough to admit that very well might not have been the case.

As it was, she'd stood by for weeks as Marc's life became a nightmare. As the insurance company hounded him, refusing to pay because they were convinced the entire thing was an inside job. That he was guilty of fraud and a myriad other crimes. That he'd done the entire thing for the money, and as some sick kind of publicity stunt.

He'd kept most of it from her, but she'd seen. How could she not when he was growing more haggard, more worried with every day that passed. And when the cops, at the insurance agency's behest, started looking at him and Nic, she'd known she couldn't keep quiet any longer.

She'd talked her father into returning the jewels—largely because he'd known she would steal them back if she had to—and then brought them to Bijoux headquarters in the most complicated reverse heist that—she was sure—had ever been pulled off.

The insurance company, the cops, Marc's board of directors—none of them had known what had hit them. And they still didn't—except for Marc, who she had confessed everything to.

And who had returned her grand gesture by kicking her out of his life without a backward glance.

She'd known it could happen before she told him—she had been lying to him for weeks, after all, while he went through hell. While the company he'd worked so hard to build had begun falling apart piece by piece. But there was a part of her that still hadn't expected it, still hadn't been ready for it. How could she have been when her love for him was so absolute, so boundless, that there was nothing he could have done that would have made her turn her back on him?

And now he'd turned his back on her again. Even after everything she'd done to create a new, legitimate life for herself. As she'd wandered the streets six years ago, she'd promised herself that she would turn her life around. That she would become someone better, someone that no one could ever accuse, ever toss aside like that, again.

She'd done it, too. She'd given up being a jewel thief when she met Marc, and once her father had died she'd given up all connections to that life—her friendships, her apartment, even her name. She'd built a new life instead, one where she could use her expertise to help, to teach, instead of to harm.

She'd done it for herself, because it had been important to her to make amends for everything she'd done. And, she realized as she walked the lonely stretch of beach watching the sky slowly turn the inky purple of twilight, she'd done it to impress Marc, too. Though she'd never sought him out, never told him who she had become, there was a part of her that had always believed that if he knew—if he found her—he'd accept the new Isa and forget the pain and the disloyalty and damage of the past.

She hadn't let herself acknowledge any of those hidden hopes until this moment, however, and now that she had, all they brought was more of the crippling pain she'd sworn she'd leave behind.

Because he didn't believe in the new her.

He didn't believe that she had changed at all.

The magnitude of the pain made her want to whimper, to cry. Why, she wanted to shout to the unsympathetic sea, why was there always more pain?

She kept walking, head bowed against the cold rolling in as darkness descended over the roiling sea. The wind picked up, blew her hair around her face, snuck inside the thin blouse that was no protection at all. It creeped inside, bringing the cold under her skin. Bringing it all the way to her bones.

And still she walked. And still, as she looked out at the waves crashing against the shore, all she could see was him.

Eyes shadowed.

Skin pale.

Jaw tight.

Fists clenched.

He'd been all but seething with rage, with betrayal, with the past that lay between them like a wasteland.

She'd known better. Had known not to take this job, not to do him this favor. Everything inside her had screamed that it was a bad idea. And yet, she'd done it anyway. How could she not have, when he'd needed her? When—despite how it had ended six years ago—she'd once loved

him with everything inside her? With her heart, her soul,
her entire being.

When—and she hated to admit it almost as much as
she hated that it was true, that it would always be true—
she loved him still.

It was because she loved him that the pain was so cat-
astrophic.

Oh, the trip she'd just taken down memory lane had
been a bitter one, filled with all the mistakes she couldn't
change. But the pain of that didn't come close to the pain
she'd felt seeing the look on Marc's face as he'd demanded
to know if she had stolen from him again. As he'd ordered
her, voice blank and eyes dead, to get out of his office. Out
of his building.

Out of his life.

Just the memory had her breath hiccupping in her throat
and tears blooming in her eyes. She told herself she wasn't
crying, that it was just the sharpness of the wind that had
her eyes stinging and her chest aching.

She didn't buy it, though.

She wasn't much of a crier—could count on one hand
the number of times she'd cried in her adult life—but right
here, right now, she couldn't *not* feel the agony and the de-
feat of what could have been.

She couldn't not cry.

She didn't know how long she stood staring out at the
vast and endless ocean.

Long enough for the tide to roll in and over her toes,
across her feet, up her calves.

Long enough for stars to twinkle against the darkness
of the night sky.

More than long enough for her tears to dry and her
heart to crack wide-open as the truth settled over her like
a mantle. Like a weight she couldn't bear.

Marc would never believe in her. Even if he found proof that she hadn't stolen those diamonds, he still wouldn't trust her. No matter what she did, no matter how much she'd changed her life, no matter how much she tried to convince him that she wasn't the person she'd once been, it wouldn't matter. He would see only what he wanted to see, believe only what he'd always believed.

It was a bitter pill to swallow, one that shattered the last vestiges of hope she hadn't even realized she'd been holding on to. But it was also the catalyst she needed to get moving again, the impetus that got her started on the long walk back to Bijoux's headquarters—and her car.

And if she cried the whole way back, well then, nobody needed to know but her...

Eighteen

Marc kept his staff working well into the night, trying to find out what had happened to the diamonds. Or, more accurately, trying to find proof that Isa had stolen them. Not because he planned to press charges but because he wanted to know.

No, not wanted. Needed. He *needed* to know. Needed the vindication that came with being proven right. He needed to know that the look on her face—in her eyes—as he'd gone off on her had been as fake as the tender words she'd whispered to him while they made love.

Because if that look wasn't fake— He shut the thought down fast. No, he wasn't going there. Wasn't going to think, even for a second, that he had made a mistake. Because if he let that idea in now, he'd never get it out of his head again. And he wanted to believe it so badly, wanted so much for Isa to be innocent, that he was afraid he would convince himself she was, even if she wasn't.

Or worse, he would convince himself that the theft didn't matter at all.

It hadn't been big diamonds, wouldn't cost his company much of anything, really, except the annoyance and manpower that came with trying to figure out how the theft had been accomplished.

He'd been over the tapes himself. He'd had Nic and Lisa and his most trusted security people go over them, too. He'd examined every second Isa had been in the vault, had studied every drawer she'd opened, every diamond she'd looked at. And he couldn't see it. Couldn't find where— or how—she'd done it.

And he needed to know how because he was never going to know why. They'd spent the past three nights making love and it had felt so good, so right. They'd fallen into old routines, old patterns of conversation, so easily. As if the six years he'd spent without her hadn't happened. As if the whole debacle back in New York was just a nightmare and not the sad, awful truth that had woken him up in the middle of the night for years.

When he thought about going back to that loneliness, thought about the fact that he would never hold Isa in his arms again, it made him crazy. Made him want to grab her and shake her all over again.

How could she do this?

Why would she do this?

How could the money from fencing the diamonds be more important to her than what they had between them?

Maybe that was the problem. Maybe he was only imagining that there were feelings under the heat. Maybe, when he'd been falling for her all over again, she'd only been using him. Only been looking for a way to get back at him for the way he'd kicked her out all those years ago.

It made sense—it really did. As long as he didn't take

into account how hard she'd worked these past few days to help him debunk that ridiculous *LA Times* article. Or how her arms had felt around him after they'd made love, so warm and sexy and perfect.

But if all that mattered to her was the thrill of the boost, why had she held him so tenderly? Why had she gone so high, so deep, when he made love to her? Why had she given herself to him so completely?

The questions were driving him crazy, the lack of understanding made him hurt in a way he hadn't let himself experience in six long years.

Furious, frustrated, completely fed up with himself and the entire situation, he turned back to his computer. Pulled up the video footage for the third time that night. And once again, watched every second of film showing Isa in the vault.

Every single second.

Most of it was boring, with nothing happening except Isa studying the diamonds under a microscope and triple-checking the serial numbers. But the times she moved, the times she crossed the vault to get a new drawer or to put one away or, ostensibly, only to stretch, he watched those the most intently.

Because he was looking for the theft, he told himself. He wanted to know when she'd dropped the diamonds into her pocket and how she'd gotten them out of the vault, out of the building. But the sad truth was, even with everything that had happened, for most of the video he just found himself watching her.

The fluid way she walked.

The way her hips swayed with each step.

The way her hair curled over her shoulders, caressed her breasts.

And damn, this so wasn't helping. It wasn't helping

him find whatever he'd missed and it sure as hell wasn't helping him forget what it felt like to touch Isa's beautiful body, to hold her in his arms as he slipped inside her.

He reached for his mouse, scrolled the video back several minutes and promised himself that this time he would pay attention. This time he wouldn't be distracted by thoughts of what she looked like and smelled like and tasted like.

Except he was only a minute into the video when a knock sounded on his office door. He froze the screen, and even though it was ridiculous, he couldn't help feeling like a kid who'd been caught watching porn. The fact that Isa had all her clothes on and was doing nothing more than counting diamonds didn't make him any less guilty.

Shoving his chair back from his desk, he walked to the door. Pulled it open. And found Bob standing there, looking as close to frantic as he'd ever seen his security chief look.

Marc's stomach sank even as he stepped aside so Bob could enter. "What's wrong now?"

"There's a problem with the video," he responded, walking around Marc's desk so that he was stationed in front of his laptop. "Can you pull up your email?"

"What kind of problem?" he demanded, already logging in and opening the first email on the list.

"There's a time lapse." Bob clicked on the attachment, then waited impatiently for the footage to download.

"A time lapse?"

"The feed in the vault was cut for a period of approximately seven minutes."

"From which camera?" Marc demanded, impatience thrumming through him.

"From all of them."

"Excuse me?"

Bob paled at his tone. "That's what it looks like, at least. Every camera in and outside the vault has a seven-minute time lapse."

"And no one noticed that the feed had been cut? Where the hell was Security?"

"That's the thing. I don't think those seven minutes were cut out until after the theft—the footage was recorded, then deleted."

"So, again, I'm asking you. Where the hell was Security?" Marc demanded with a glare. "People are paid to do nothing but watch those monitors twenty-four hours a day."

"That's what I'm trying to figure out. We don't yet know if they fed other footage into the digital stream, but that's what I'm surmising. At this point, there's no other explanation that makes sense."

"Someone hacked into my system—my specially designed, one-of-a-kind, cover-all-the-bases system—and took control of every camera in or around the vault. That's what you're telling me?"

"Essentially, yes."

"And no one noticed."

"That's not totally true. We noticed."

"Not until after the theft!" he snapped, then bent down to look at the dates at the bottom of the footage. "This happened on Monday?"

"Yes."

"How did they hack in?"

"We're still working on that."

"Work harder. And get Geoffrey and Max on it. I want an answer—tonight."

"I get that you're upset, Marc, but we're doing the best we can. The work was so good that it's damn impressive one of my guys even caught—"

"It will be damn impressive when you find the weakness he exploited and eliminate it. Until then, it's only sloppy." He stared at the screen grimly. "On every single one of our parts."

Bob didn't have much more to say after that—not that Marc blamed him. He was furious, absolutely seething now that he knew some thief had hacked into his computer system. He had two of the best internet security guys in the world on his payroll and some jackass had managed to completely hijack his security feed?

Enraged didn't begin to cover what Marc was feeling.

He spent the next few hours snapping at his employees as every single one of them—including him—searched for the weakness. For how it had been done. By the time midnight rolled around, they still hadn't found the weakness in the operating system that had allowed this to happen. Which made him—and his computer security guys—even more suspicious.

Usually, hackers and thieves didn't care if you knew how they got in. They'd already gotten what they wanted, after all, so why should it matter to them if you closed the hole after they'd left? But this person had made sure to cover their tracks so well that Marc couldn't help wondering if this was the first time it had happened—or if it was merely the first time the thief had gotten caught? Maybe the person had been stealing from them for quite some time, taking only a couple small, inconsequential stones every few months, all in an effort to stay off the radar.

They only inventoried the vault fully twice a year. So if this hadn't been going on very long—if they'd only caught it because of the internal audit they were running—

He finally let himself acknowledge what had been racing around his mind for hours. He finally let himself admit how thoroughly he'd screwed up.

The thought had him sweating, had his stomach clenching and his heart beating too fast. Because if this was an inside job, which he and his security guys thought it was, and it had been going on for a while, then…then there was no way Isa was responsible for it.

He'd blamed her, cut her out, and she hadn't done it.

The thought made him sick, especially if he let himself think about what she'd looked like after he'd confronted her. How shocked, how hurt…how devastated.

She'd looked like he'd felt, as if her whole world had been yanked out from under her. Again.

And he'd done it to her. Just like he'd done it to her six years ago. He'd let his anger and his pride and his distrust get the better of him, again. The fact that he'd actually let her collect her things this time didn't make him feel any better about himself as a human being—or as a boyfriend.

With a curse, he shoved back from the conference room table they'd been using as command central.

Nic, Bob, Geoffrey—and all the others gathered there—stared at him in trepidation. It made him realize just how angry, and vile, he'd been to all of them since the theft was discovered.

"Go home," he told them gruffly. "We'll pick this up tomorrow."

"Home?" Geoffrey repeated, as if it was a concept utterly foreign to him.

"We've been at this for days, pretty much nonstop. Go home, get some sleep, relax a little. We'll pick it up in the morning."

"Who are you?" Nic demanded. But Marc noticed that his brother shoved away from the table pretty damn quickly.

"The damage has already been done, right? I want two extra guards stationed on the vault floor—one right outside the vault and an extra guard running patrol and—weakness or not—the vault should be okay for another night, right?"

They nearly tripped over themselves agreeing with him.

"Okay, then. Go home and I'll see you back here at 7 a.m."

Before they could say anything else, he turned on his heel and strode out. He had something important to do and it was already days—years—overdue.

Nineteen

Isa woke up from a fitful sleep at the first round of violent pounding on her front door. Fumbling for her phone—just in case she had to call 9-1-1—she glanced at the time. One o'clock. Who on earth was at her door at one in the morning?

Snatching her robe from the chair by her bed, she shrugged it on as she made her way cautiously to her front door. A look through the window told her Marc was her middle-of-the-night visitor. He looked better than he had any right to, especially considering how haggard and exhausted she knew she must look.

Their gazes met through the glass and for a second she was mesmerized by the look in his eyes. But then her sense of self-preservation kicked in and she yanked her gaze away—at the same time she took a couple steps back. She didn't want to see him, didn't want to talk to him or even look at him. Not now, when the wounds were still so fresh. Not now, when it still hurt to breathe.

Marc must have read her intention on her face, though, because the pounding doubled. And then he started to call to her. "Open the door, Isa. Please. I just want to talk to you."

She shook her head even though he couldn't see her anymore, backed away a few more steps. She didn't want to see him—couldn't see him. It hurt too much. Even knowing that she was responsible for his distrust, that she'd brought all of this on herself with how she'd behaved six years ago, didn't make the pain any easier to bear.

"Damn it, Isa, please! I just want to talk to you."

But she didn't want to talk to him. She couldn't handle any more accusations, couldn't handle him looking at her as if she was trash. Or worse, as if she'd ripped out his heart. She hadn't done it, hadn't stolen the jewels, but that didn't make her feel any less guilty. Not when she'd been responsible for so much of what had happened to him, and Bijoux, six years ago.

"Isa! Please! I'm sorry." For the first time, his voice cracked. "I'm so sorry. Please let me in."

It hurt her to hear him sound so broken. Before she could think better of it, she cleared her throat, told him, "Go away, Marc. This isn't helping anyone."

"Isa, please. You have every right to hate me, every right to be angry with me. But please, I'm begging of you, don't send me away."

She didn't know how to respond to that. He sounded so different from the man she'd spoken to on Wednesday that it broke her heart all over again. She couldn't stand to hear the pain in his voice, couldn't stand to hear him beg when she'd been the one to hurt him so badly that he'd never be able to trust her again.

Her body moved before her mind made a conscious decision, sliding the dead bolt back and taking the chain off and opening the door to him. To Marc. The only man she'd ever loved.

The only man she'd ever hurt.

"I'm sorry," he told her the moment they were face-to-face. "I'm so sorry."

"It's okay," she told him, stepping back to let him in the house. "I assume you've found the thief?"

"No." He shook his head. "Not yet."

His words didn't make any sense. "I don't understand. If you don't know who did it, why are you here?"

"Because I know it wasn't you. Because I'm an asshole who let the pain of the past blind him to the woman you've become, the woman you are now."

She stared at him stupidly. She could hear what he was saying, but she couldn't comprehend it. Not when it was so far from what she'd expected. So far from anything in their experience so far.

"How do you know it wasn't me?"

"I know because I know you."

"You knew me three days ago. That didn't seem to matter."

"Three days ago, I was a blind, bullheaded ass who was too busy trying to hide his wounds to think things through."

"What things?"

"Everything. The idea that you would steal from Bijoux is ridiculous. And if you did, I'd like to think you'd have better taste than to take a few mundane diamonds that don't matter much to anyone."

"Seriously?" she demanded, feeling as if she'd fallen down some kind of rabbit hole. For the first time, anger cut through the grief. "That's why you're here? Because the thief's taste wasn't good enough, therefore it couldn't be me who did it?"

"No," he said, grabbing her elbows in his big hands and pulling her close. She wanted to shrug him off, wanted to back away, but her body yearned for his touch, his warmth. "I'm here because I made a mistake. Because I know you wouldn't steal from me, wouldn't hurt me that way. And because I want—need—to tell you how sorry I am for hurting you the way I did. Three days ago and six years ago.

"I've been an ass, more concerned with protecting myself than with protecting you, and that's inexcusable."

"It's not your job to protect me—"

"That's bullshit. I love you, Isa. I love you more than I can ever tell you, more than you'll ever believe considering my actions. And it is absolutely my job to protect you and take care of you and make you understand just how precious you are. And I've totally screwed all that up."

He shook his head, looking so disgusted with himself that she nearly cried at the injustice of it. "I did terrible things—"

"No, you didn't. You were young, and torn between two men you loved—neither of whom deserved you. I'm sorry, Isa. I'm so sorry."

He pulled her even closer then and rested his forehead against hers. "I don't deserve you. Don't deserve your forgiveness and I sure as hell don't deserve your love. But I want it, Isa. I want it so bad."

His words turned her brain to mush, and her heart into a ray of light. She threw her arms around him, pulled him close even as harsh sobs ripped through her.

"Don't cry, baby," he said, holding her tightly. "Please don't cry. I'll make it up to you if you let me. I'll—"

She kissed him then, with all the pent-up passion and love and fear and forgiveness she had inside herself. She kissed him and kissed him and kissed him.

And he kissed her back.

Minutes, hours—days—passed before they finally came up for air. His hands on her cheeks, her arms around his neck. Their gazes locked together. "I'm sorry," Marc said again. "I'm so sorry."

"So am I."

"You don't have anything—"

"I do," she told him, pressing kisses along his strong and stubbled jawline. "You aren't the only one who made mistakes. I messed up six years ago, badly, and I don't blame you for thinking I messed up again."

"You didn't, though. I know that even if we never find the thief—"

"Oh, we'll find him," she declared adamantly. "No way is some jerk getting away with stealing from the man I love."

Marc laughed even as he hugged her closer. "You sound so fierce."

"I feel fierce," she said, tugging him down the hall toward her bedroom.

"Do you?" He crooked that brow that always made her crazy.

"I do. And as soon as it's morning, we're going back to Bijoux and we're going to start figuring who did this to you. To us. Together."

"Together." He bent, pressed his own kisses against her lips, her cheek, her forehead, her eyes. "I like the sound of that."

"So do I." She held him tight. "I love you, Marc. I love you so much."

"I love you, too. I always have and I always will."

His words reached inside, thawing out the last of the cold that had lingered there since that long-ago night in Manhattan. And as she pulled him into her room—into her bed—she couldn't help thinking that it had all been worth it. To get here, to this moment, she'd trade a million diamonds, go through whatever pain it took.

Because Marc was worth it. And so was the life they would build together.

* * * * *

Don't miss Nic's story
PURSUED

Coming October 2015
only from
New York Times *bestselling author Tracy Wolff*
and
Harlequin Desire!

If you're on Twitter, tell us what you think of
Harlequin Desire! #harlequindesire

COMING NEXT MONTH FROM

HARLEQUIN *Desire*

Available October 6, 2015

#2401 A CONTRACT ENGAGEMENT • by Maya Banks

In this reader-favorite story, billionaire businessman Evan Ross has special terms for Celia Taylor, the sexy ad executive desperate to seal a career-making deal. But she's turning the tables with demands of her own...

#2402 STRANDED WITH THE BOSS

Billionaires and Babies • by Elizabeth Lane

Early tragedy led billionaire Dragan to steer clear of children. But could a spunky redhead—who's suing his company!—and her twin toddlers melt his frozen heart when they're stranded together in a winter cabin?

#2403 PURSUED

The Diamond Tycoons • by Tracy Wolff

Nic Durand had a one-night stand with the reporter exposing corruption in his company. Now she's having his child. She may be set on bringing him down, but he'll pursue her until he has her right where he wants her!

#2404 A ROYAL TEMPTATION

Dynasties: The Montoros • by Charlene Sands

When Princess Portia Lindstrom shows up at his coronation, it's love at first sight for King Juan Carlos. But soon her family's explosive secret could force the unwavering royal to choose between his country's future and his own.

#2405 FALLING FOR HER FAKE FIANCÉ

The Beaumont Heirs • by Sarah M. Anderson

Frances Beaumont needs a fortune. CEO Ethan Logan needs a Beaumont to give him credibility when he takes over the family brewery. Can this engagement of convenience lead to the real deal?

#2406 HIS 24-HOUR WIFE

The Hawke Brothers • by Rachel Bailey

Their spontaneous Vegas marriage should have ended the day after it began! But when they partner on a project, Adam and Callie must pretend they're still together to avoid a high-profile scandal. Will they soon want more than a short-term solution?

YOU CAN FIND MORE INFORMATION ON UPCOMING HARLEQUIN® TITLES, FREE EXCERPTS AND MORE AT WWW.HARLEQUIN.COM.

HDCNM0915

REQUEST YOUR FREE BOOKS!
2 FREE NOVELS PLUS 2 FREE GIFTS!

⊞ HARLEQUIN®

Desire

ALWAYS POWERFUL, PASSIONATE AND PROVOCATIVE

YES! Please send me 2 FREE Harlequin® Desire novels and my 2 FREE gifts (gifts are worth about $10). After receiving them, if I don't wish to receive any more books, I can return the shipping statement marked "cancel." If I don't cancel, I will receive 6 brand-new novels every month and be billed just $4.55 per book in the U.S. or $5.24 per book in Canada. That's a savings of at least 13% off the cover price! It's quite a bargain! Shipping and handling is just 50¢ per book in the U.S. and 75¢ per book in Canada.* I understand that accepting the 2 free books and gifts places me under no obligation to buy anything. I can always return a shipment and cancel at any time. Even if I never buy another book, the two free books and gifts are mine to keep forever.

225/326 HDN GH2P

Name _____ (PLEASE PRINT) _____

Address _____ Apt. # _____

City _____ State/Prov. _____ Zip/Postal Code _____

Signature (if under 18, a parent or guardian must sign)

Mail to the **Reader Service:**

IN U.S.A.: P.O. Box 1867, Buffalo, NY 14240-1867
IN CANADA: P.O. Box 609, Fort Erie, Ontario L2A 5X3

Want to try two free books from another line?
Call 1-800-873-8635 or visit www.ReaderService.com.

* Terms and prices subject to change without notice. Prices do not include applicable taxes. Sales tax applicable in N.Y. Canadian residents will be charged applicable taxes. Offer not valid in Quebec. This offer is limited to one order per household. Not valid for current subscribers to Harlequin Desire books. All orders subject to credit approval. Credit or debit balances in a customer's account(s) may be offset by any other outstanding balance owed by or to the customer. Please allow 4 to 6 weeks for delivery. Offer available while quantities last.

Your Privacy—The Reader Service is committed to protecting your privacy. Our Privacy Policy is available online at www.ReaderService.com or upon request from the Reader Service.

We make a portion of our mailing list available to reputable third parties that offer products we believe may interest you. If you prefer that we not exchange your name with third parties, or if you wish to clarify or modify your communication preferences, please visit us at www.ReaderService.com/consumerchoice or write to us at Reader Service Preference Service, P.O. Box 9062, Buffalo, NY 14240-9062. Include your complete name and address.

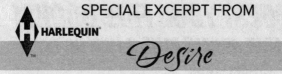
He was the most beautiful man she'd ever seen.

Desi Maddox knew that sounded excessive, melodramatic even, but the longer she stood there staring at him, the more convinced she became.

His emerald gaze met hers over the sea of people stretching between them and her knees trembled. Her heart raced and her palms grew damp with the force of her reaction to a man she'd never seen before and more than likely would never see again.

It was a deflating thought, and exactly what she needed to remind herself of what she was doing here among the best and brightest of San Diego's high society. Scoping out hot men was definitely not what her boss was paying her for. Unfortunately.

Wanting to free up her hands, she turned to place her glass on the empty tray of yet another passing waiter. As she turned back, though, her eyes once again met dark green ones. And, this time, the man they belonged to was only a couple of feet away.

She didn't know whether to run or rejoice.

In the end, she just stared—stupefied—up into his too-gorgeous face and tried to think of something to say that wouldn't make her sound like a total moron. Her usually quick mind was a blank, filled with nothing but images of high cheekbones. Shaggy black hair that fell over his forehead. Wickedly gleaming eyes. The sensuous mouth turned up in a wide, charming smile. Broad shoulders. And height. He was so tall she was forced to look up, despite the fact that she stood close to six feet in her four-inch heels.

"You look thirsty," he said, and—of course—his voice matched the rest of him. All deep and dark and husky and wickedly amused. "I'm Nic, by the way."

"I'm Desi." She held out her hand. He took it, but instead of shaking it as she'd expected, he held it as he gently stroked his thumb across the back.

It was so soft, so intimate, so not what she'd been expecting, that for long seconds she didn't know what to do. A tiny voice inside her was whispering for her to escape from the attraction holding them in thrall. But it was drowned out by the heat, the *sizzle*, that arced between them like lightning.

"Would you like to dance, Desi?" he asked.

She should say no. But even as the thought occurred to her, even knowing that she might very well get burned before the night was over, she nodded.

Don't miss PURSUED
by New York Times *bestselling author Tracy Wolff,*
available October 2015 wherever
Harlequin® Desire books and ebooks are sold.

www.Harlequin.com